Marie

Also by Madeleine Bourdouxhe

La Femme de Gilles
Sous le Pont Mirabeau
A Nail, A Rose

Marie

Madeleine Bourdouxhe

TRANSLATED AND WITH AN AFTERWORD BY
FAITH EVANS

DAUNT BOOKS

This edition first published in 2016 by
Daunt Books
83 Marylebone High Street
London W1U 4QW

3

First published as *A la Recherche de Marie* in 1943
by Editions Libris, Brussels

First published in Great Britain in 1997
by Bloomsbury Publishing

A CIP catalogue record for this title is
available from the British Library.

ISBN 978-1-907970-76-4

Typeset by Marsha Swan

Printed and bound by TJ International

www.dauntbookspublishing.co.uk

Marie

CHAPTER ONE

'MARIE, ARE YOU READY?'

She could tell Jean was cross by the way he opened the bedroom door. She moved sharply away from the window, pretending to be busy, closing the curtains: 'Yes, I'm ready … best to keep the curtains drawn in this heat.'

'I've been waiting for half an hour, you know.'

She looked at his angry face and followed him out of the room.

Marie hadn't even done her hair. She'd entered the room, looked through the open window, spotted a boat in the sea. She'd moved forward to see it more clearly and then stayed where she was, resting her head on the window-frame. She'd heard the din of the old bus that ran through the village, the reverberating noise of a motor-boat on its way into port, the cries of a group of children as they ran up to the harbour.

The boat that had attracted her attention had long since moved out of sight, and silence had returned. A whiff of resin drifted up from below.

They were the only people on the stairs. She put her arm round his shoulders: 'Are you cross with me?'

In the ground-floor lobby she stopped for a moment in front of the mirror. 'Is my hair all right?' Her chignon needed attention and a dark lock was falling too low over the right side of her forehead, just as it had before she'd gone upstairs.

'Yes, it's fine. You took your time, but you look great.'

She didn't argue. He wasn't very observant: so keen was he to get off that he must have looked at her without really seeing her at all. And she had made him wait for half an hour, it was true …

As they were leaving the house, she said: 'It's so hot! You'll really enjoy your swim.'

'What about you?'

'I don't know, I'll tell you when I've seen the water.'

'You always say that, but you never go in!'

THE ROAD is white, dry, without shade. They enter into the heat, cutting across it without saying a word. Marie's dress is faintly transparent in the sunlight, and the outline of her long supple legs shows through the cloth; in the shifting light her hair looks chestnut, red, blonde. Head high, she blinks her eyes and wrinkles her forehead; from time to time she raises her big, beautiful hands to shield her face.

They come to a narrower road leading directly to the sea. They walk very close to each other, on the right-hand side of the road, in the partial shade offered by some young cypresses. Marie's hair returns to a more consistent colour, her face relaxes and her eyes are more clearly visible: those distant eyes that seem to rise up to things with a kind of indifference. Then suddenly the road stops, runs into the beach; the light regains its searing intensity.

AS THEY SAT close to each other on the sand, Jean started to remove his sandals.

'Do wait a little before going in,' Marie said. 'It's too soon since you finished lunch ...'

Turning towards his wife he looked into her anxious eyes. 'Two hours – that's enough! But if you want me to wait I will. I don't want you to start panicking the moment I walk into the water.'

Marie moved nearer to him and closed her eyes, leaning her head on his shoulder. Jean is right next to me. Jean, the only man I love in the whole world ... I lov heart was drowning in an infinite tenderness, and her mind began to create strange pictures. She was going with Jean into a place full of warm, intimate shadows; he was pushing her gently towards a table. Lightly touching her bare arm with his hand, he held it there for a long time before letting go. 'Do you want to dance, my darling?' He took her up to a raised, narrow dance floor, put his arms around her, almost lifting her up, transporting her to the rhythm of some popular,

sensual music. (She hesitated: was it mediocre music? Yes –
the music has to be sensuous, vulgar, the more mediocre the
better.) How well they were dancing; and that loving gesture
of his, lightly brushing her forehead with his lips!

Marie, sitting on the beach, snuggled even further into
Jean's shoulder. They were dancing so very close that his
happiness must surely equal her own: he too must want
their embraces to last forever.

'It's so hot, my love ... don't cling to me like that!'

Marie disentangled herself. Closing her eyes again, she
raised her knees and rested her head upon them. He wanted
their embraces to last forever ... they were still dancing. On
the way back to the table he looked at her and said, in a voice
sweet with promise: 'Shall we go home?'

MARIE LOOKS UP and her eyes rediscover, without actually
taking them in, the water, the boats, the sand and the scattering of light on the sea. She remembers the conversations
she has had with friends – pointless, irritating conversations
that are always the same but in which she participates none
the less. She hears Lucy saying: 'Marie, you love your husband
very deeply; you've managed to find complete fulfilment in
your love; you are the only one amongst us who really knows
what happiness is.' Smiling, she always replies: 'Yes, it's true.'
And now, recalling that exchange, that same mysterious smile
returns to her mouth. She turns round and stretches full out,
her face towards the ground; the smile has disappeared. 'What
is happiness?' she asks herself. 'What does happiness mean?'

'Whether you want me to or not, it's time I went for my swim!' Jean shouts, taking off.

SHE GETS UP immediately, and looks for him anxiously in the direction of the sea. He's a bad swimmer, but nothing will stop him from going further out than he should. When she finally spots him her eyes do not leave him – she follows his every movement. He dives, and something in her tenses up; she holds her breath until his head reappears a bit further on, gleaming with water between the waves. He starts to come in; the water is now only up to his waist. He waves at her and, hands on hips, stands watching the other bathers.

Taking advantage of this moment of respite Marie sits down again and looks to her left. She sees someone sitting on a rock; he's only half visible, but from the rear he looks very young. He is getting ready for a swim. His hair is black and rather untidy, and his shoulders are lean, though firm and strong. Head down, he walks along the pebbles, then he jumps up and takes a few steps up the beach, towards where she is sitting.

He raises his head, and her eyes meet his.

Marie is the first to blink and turn away: where is Jean? There he is, among the other bathers. She turns to the left again. The young man is now stretched out on the sand, face towards the sun. Just as she thought, he has slender, strong, tanned shoulders, and long, muscular legs, even browner than hers. Slowly, her eyes take in the full extent of his body as he lies there, following all the contours, scrutinising his young flesh.

He raises his arms and crosses his wrists over his face to protect his eyes from the sun. How young he is! What enthusiasms, what hopes, what expectations lie behind those closed eyelids?

Suddenly she hears Jean's voice. 'I'm hungry! I'll get dressed and then we'll go and have a snack!'

He runs towards the rocks, stopping at the very point where Marie first noticed the young man. She sees Jean, in the same frame, making the same movements: it's practically the same scene, but touched with another halo. Jean leans over and stands up, remaining still for a moment, offering his bare chest to the sun. Inclining her head, she watches him, watches all those gestures that she knows so well and so intimately. Reality tamed: a tender halo emerging from sweetness, from the warmth of the familiar, from someone you love.

And before? The unknown young man who thought he was invisible between two rocks? Another moment, another halo ... A reality to guess at, to seize on, to make your own. The realm of the possible; the fascination and excitement of a new world.

Marie swivels round again, letting her gaze rest for a moment on the young, immobile body. Lives which form life, worlds which give shape to the world ... Her face lights up, as if she had suddenly rediscovered a memory. Folding her arms on the sand, she completely buries her head in them and, in the narrow chapel of her crossed arms, she breathes her own breath: 'Are you there, Marie? Yes, I'm still here, quite alone in my own arms ... Marie!'

JEAN AND MARIE had taken to sitting on the balcony of the hotel where, every day at the same time, you could see the same holidaymakers sitting with a coffee, a cup of tea, a *menthe*. It wasn't as hot as earlier on, but as the afternoon came to an end, everything remained steeped in torpor, retaining the heat of the whole day. There was something ineffable around Marie that was making her happy. Jean was next to her, serving her coffee, giving her a cigarette: an intimate little scene, on the balcony of a hotel, overlooking the sea.

A large parasol protected the table, and in the shadowy light Jean's face showed up clearly, those rather slack features that could sometimes tense into irritability. She watched him run his broad hands, the little fingers shadowed by down, through his fair hair, which the holiday sun had lightened even more. There was definitely strength in his character – or rather, there were bouts of strength. Jean had a way of claiming his due, or more than his due: a somewhat egotistical way of deciding, of drinking, of eating, of sitting, of occupying his place.

'You're very quiet, Marie?'

'I'm watching you.'

He smiled and filled his cup, adding a cube of sugar. Turning towards her again he asked: 'Do you love me?'

'I love you.'

She had spoken quietly, deeply. She lowered her eyes and, pausing a moment as if she was thinking about it, looked back at him again and repeated, in a more normal, stronger voice: 'I love you. Yes, I love you.'

Laughing, she went on: 'You've known that for such a very long time!'

'Six years – it's beginning to add up, isn't it?'

And he laughed, too, clasping her slender wrist a little too tightly.

A group of young women carrying tennis rackets came up. Marie exclaimed: 'What, you've been playing in this heat?'

'The courts are in shade, and we take a break between each game. You ought to come with us, Marie. What about tomorrow?'

'Fancy asking Marie to come with us! Don't go on at her: Jean doesn't play tennis and it's unthinkable that Marie, the most loving, the most faithful woman of them all, would ever abandon him for an afternoon!'

Marie smiled, calmly. She watched the young women, she watched Jean, and then, as if absentminded or indifferent, let her gaze wander to the sea, to the horizon, fixing it upon that uncertain infinity.

Jean was all attention: 'What do you want to drink? Do join us.'

'No, we're on our way back. Are you staying in the hotel this evening? We'll come and find you there.'

Alone again, Jean and Marie sat on, in an easy silence.

Gradually the weather had changed. The sky was still clear over the sea but over the village it grew dull, and threatening clouds began to appear above the land. They heard a heavy, far-off rumble and a short while later, another, less muffled rumble echoed in the nearby mountains. Marie looked worried. 'Do you think it's coming in this direction?' she asked.

'I don't think so, the wind seems to be coming from—'

A third, louder rumble interrupted him. He turned towards Marie and made a face: 'Poor Marie – you'd better get ready to suffer ...'

She tried to laugh. She saw the hotel waiters fold up the tablecloths and close the parasols; then there was a brief, dull flash of lightning, like a reflection. She raised a pathetic, taut face towards the sky, then looked down again, wilting with fear. 'Let's go back,' she said. 'You know how frightened I get, I hate thunderstorms.'

He urged her to wait, promised her it would soon be over. She sat in silence, doing her best to stifle her unease.

After several spaced-out drops the rain stopped abruptly; the only sound was another clap of thunder, but a long way away. Marie's face relaxed. The sun suddenly reappeared. She regained her cheerfulness and suggested a walk along the harbour.

Marie took Jean's arm, and the two of them walked close together in the sweetness of the rediscovered sun, watching the little boats and the extended fishing rods. When Jean started talking to a fisherman Marie, still holding her husband's arm, turned towards the mountains. Behind the high bare peaks she imagined a deluge of water, noise, and streaks of lightning; she saw herself rushing down those dry slopes, looking up at the flashing light, her face pitched against the cold, hard storm, entirely alone.

Gasping a little, she turned back towards the harbour. Her eyes were still sparkling, but they gradually lost their brightness and finally softened as they came to rest, calmly and tenderly, upon Jean.

In the evening the friends were reunited in the garden of the hotel. Jean, in high spirits, was chatting with Lucy and two other young women.

'I'm going as far as the road,' Marie said, so softly that the others barely noticed.

THE LEAVES ON THE TREES along the road are completely still; the smell of pines, overheated by the day, still rises in waves, but the night is full and fresh, and the earth has eased up. Marie reaches the road that she took that afternoon with Jean and follows it to the end.

It is hard to see, now, where the beach ends and the sea begins. She goes on walking; she hears the lapping of the water against a boat. She has never tried untying a craft and rowing it in the sea; she does not know the precise movements that are required. But she is suddenly overtaken by curiosity.

Under the thrust of her hands the boat slides along the sand, and finally floats. She gets in, takes the oars, and fumbles clumsily in the water. It's hard … If Jean was there, he would row vigorously and the boat would move quickly. He would say: 'Look at me!' They would go out a little further and would stay sitting in the boat, for a long time, leaning against each other. But Jean is not here. He is of less concern to her now than the sea, the boat and its oars. And the oars must be raised – yes, like that – and then forced backwards, plunged into the water, brought back, raised again, and while this is happening you must lean your chest forward, then straighten up again; you must embrace the rhythm so as to become the very movement itself.

She is already far from the water's edge. She stops, puts the oars at ease and looks around her. How lovely the sea is! It's as though she can see the colour of the water in the night, and breathe the smell that rises up from it, for the first time in years. At that moment she is alone. And against that mixed background of smells and colours an essential truth re-emerges, with great clarity and precision. Once again she grasps its full significance, in all its weight and seriousness, as if it were a plundered secret.

Now she allows herself to move at the same pace as the water, without any sense of fear. Does it matter where is she going? Perhaps the waves will take her even further out or perhaps they will bring her gently back to the shore.

Suddenly she hears familiar voices.

'Marie! Where are you?'

'Hey, Marie! Marie, say something!'

She sits up, steers the boat towards the beach, and finds the rock that is her landmark. She jumps out and swiftly ties up the ropes. The voices go on calling. Finally she replies, and makes her way towards Jean and the young women.

'Where were you? Did you leave the road, then?'

'If we didn't know how scared you are of the water we'd have thought you'd gone out all on your own, in a boat or a canoe or something! But there was no danger of that, was there?'

'We were looking for you to take you to the harbour. Come on!'

Smiling, Marie lets herself be led away by all the arms that reach out to her.

A fishing boat had just arrived at the harbour, and everyone rushed towards it, to see the catch as it was unloaded. They joined in, passing full baskets and placing them on one of the seats that surrounded the narrow quay of this rectangular little harbour. They gathered round in a circle, questioning the fisherman and leaning over the fresh fish.

As Jean and the young women moved off Marie was about to follow them. Looking up she suddenly stood stock still; she stopped breathing, as though constricted by too tight an embrace. There he was, standing right in front of her, leaning on the back of the bench with his long adolescent hands. She saw again, through his clothing, the slim tanned shoulders, the long brown legs, the slender hips. Again they exchanged looks. How old was he? Nineteen, twenty? His eyes were solemn; twenty-two perhaps, certainly no older: the light scratch under his eyes was a sign of youth rather than maturity.

Although the fisherman now had only these two silent spectators, he went on with his explanations. Conversation soon started up again and while the boy was questioning the fisherman, Marie looked at him. And when it was her turn to do the talking, the boy's gaze rested on her. They did not speak to each other; their words merged with those of the fisherman.

'Well, all that fish will provide some good meals for tomorrow!'

They laughed together at what the fisherman had just said. Not that his remark was particularly funny – their laughter was more nervous than merry.

LATER, in the half-darkness of the bedroom, she is lying stretched out, with Jean's arms around her.

'Jean, my darling …'

She whispers in a wounded voice, her whole spirit reaching painfully towards a goal that she feels she must achieve. Something heavy and stifling takes shape, expands, rises, bursts. Marie's desperate sense of sadness dissipates and she lies there, exhausted by happiness – but a happiness that is cerebral rather than physical. Jean, barely startled by the trembling of her body, places her firmly back by his side

'Go straight to sleep now, Marie.'

Moving away from her, he turns round and is asleep. Marie wants to die. Do all men turn round and sleep like this, after making love? They probably do …

She slides to the other edge of the bed to find the cold place that is hers. She buries her tear-streaked face in the icy pillow. And she stays that way, her young animal desire still intact.

CHAPTER TWO

'HERE, JEAN, TAKE THE SUNTAN OIL.'

'What about you – still not going to use it?'

'No, I get quite brown enough without oil or sunbathing,' Marie said.

She stretched out a leg to reveal a matt brown skin marked by small scratches from stones and brambles. 'Are you planning to stay here in the garden? I want to go and take some photos ...' She had already set off, but turned round to say: 'All the same, Jean, do be careful – you have such delicate skin ... Hang on a moment, let me help you with your back.'

As she covered Jean's back with oil a very soft, tender look came into her eyes. 'There now, out of danger ... you can lie full out in the sun!' Laughing, Marie wiped her hands on the grass in the flowerbed.

SHE WALKED for a long time, following the same road – always white, dry, without shade. She went up several paths that led only to fields of olive trees, and then returned to the harbour, looking all round it with searching eyes. She retraced her steps towards the road back, then took a new path, flanked by two low walls, which ended up way down the beach, opposite a tiny island.

Now she can come to a halt, for he is there, several metres from her, sitting on a narrow promontory of rocks.

She trembles a little, then controls herself and walks on. She passes him and stops on the rocks, camera in hand, searching for the island through the lens.

'If you want to photograph the island, you'd do better to stand back a few paces. The view will be better.'

At the sound of his voice Marie steps back, almost without realising it: her whole life is in the small fragment of flesh that is her wrist, encircled by an unfamiliar hand. Then she is free again: she points the camera, works the shutter.

'A Zeiss Ikon? It's the same as mine.'

'They're good cameras …'

He has jumped down from the rocks on to the sand and holds out a helping hand. She has already taken off, expecting him to step back a bit to let her land. But he doesn't move; he catches her, and holds her close for several seconds.

They sit on the sand. They might have gone on talking; about the distant hills that unfold towards the sea, about a white villa the outline of which is visible among the cypresses. But what would have been the point? They know that there is nothing to say. They mutually accept this great silence, and the richness, the sincerity that lies within it. They also know that in that moment they are seeing everything from the same point of view and that, for both of them, that red sail on the sea stands out as clearly, as harshly, as cruelly, as the thing that is deep inside them.

They went back towards the road; pointing out a path that Marie hadn't yet taken, he said: 'That ought to be a short cut.'

'But can you be sure it leads to the village?'

Shrugging his shoulders he said: 'Don't you like taking risks?'

Marie smiled, and walked ahead of him along the path.

She was walking fast, not worrying about her bare feet inside her sandals and the sharp stones in the road. Tense and straight-backed, she went faster and faster, in spite of the heat, even though the road was getting rockier and rockier, and the slope steeper. He followed close behind her and although she managed to stay upright while stumbling on the stones, he held out his arm to help her, holding her gently by the elbow. They didn't know how long the climb would take, there was very little shade, and they were bathed in sweat. Finally they were gasping uncontrollably, totally exhausted.

'You're walking too fast … let's stop for a moment.'

As though she had not heard what he'd just said, Marie appeared to be ready to continue with this hellish journey. But holding out his arms he took her firmly by the elbow, pushed her to the right side of the road, and made her sit down, in the shade of some olive trees.

MARIE, DREAMILY WATCHING the branches of a tree criss-crossed against the sky, feels his body against her, almost on top of her, feels his strong hands slipping her clothes from her shoulders and throat, feels him caressing her damp skin.

'You're so hot ...'

Marie puts up a fight; she struggles; in one movement of her long sinewy thighs, she repulses him. He returns to the charge, backs off, tries again, and occasionally succeeds in coming to rest, motionless, on top of her. She still has too many clothes on.

'What is it? Are you afraid?'

'What would I be afraid of?'

'I don't know – of nothing.'

In a barely audible voice, anguished as a moan of pain, she says: 'Of nothing – yes, perhaps this is nothing – let me go ...'

She has rejected the tender weight of his body and is now immobile in victory. But what other struggle was coming to an end behind her closed eyelids? No more images ... A face passes to and fro over memories of six years: a familiar, adored, rather tense face.

They go back down towards the path, walking slowly, side by side, their beautiful, thwarted desire heavy between them.

He says: 'When are you leaving here?'

'In a few days.'

'And after the holidays, back to Paris?'

'Yes. What about you?'

'I'm going back tonight.'

He takes out a packet of cigarettes, offers one to her, takes one himself. He tears off a piece of paper from the packet, writes a word on it and some figures: 'There, I'm going to leave you now.'

She lets him go, then comes back and leans against the low wall that borders the road. She stays there, completely alone, lost between two shattered worlds, clasping the little scrap of paper in the palm of her feverish hand: WAGRAM 17–42.

CHAPTER THREE

A LIVING ROOM, a study, a bedroom, a kitchen. A complete little world of wood, metal, windows and materials lies ready to welcome them back, to weave once more, with every move they make, the gentle fabric of daily life.

Marie breathes in the air of an apartment that has been abandoned for a month. She touches the utensils in the kitchen, wonders at their outlines. The coffee pot and the pans have taken on the metallic odour of things not used for a while.

'Shall we go to a restaurant, Jean?'

'Let's not, surely we've had enough of eating out?'

He's right. As soon as the suitcases are through the door Jean seems pleased to be home and to have to sort out the load of circulars and papers spilling from the letter box. Washing those kitchen things is going to have to be done some time, Marie thinks, whether it's today or tomorrow. Should she wait and let the cleaner do it? No, she can't leave the whole task to a girl who comes in only two mornings a week.

The next day, after Jean had left for the office, Marie emptied the cases and put them away, introducing a degree of order into the space around her.

'Germaine, it's not worth taking the linen into the bedroom; my husband prefers to keep it in the bathroom.'

'Oh yes, that's right, Madame.'

'My husband prefers' ... 'Oh yes, Madame': a wife, a husband, a household, a Germaine. Habits interrupted, then resumed again: Marie found it oddly, abruptly disturbing. She stopped what she was doing and leaned against the piece of furniture she was dusting. She let her thoughts wander but then, fearing that they would run amok, made her way to the kitchen and began to prepare lunch.

Returning to the living room, she spread a coloured linen cloth on the table and arranged some flowers in a vase, keeping a close eye on every detail. Jean was about to come home. They would lunch together side by side in a mood of tenderness which Marie was already anticipating and which she would watch over so carefully, so attentively. She has been preserving this thing for years, and now ...

LIFE RESUMED its course, slowly, indecisively.

Thursday came round – teaching day. Marie enjoys the work, and it allows her to contribute to the household budget.

As she brings the child into the room, a lazy boy of fifteen who needs special coaching to bring him up to the level of the others, she asks him: 'Where did we get to?'

'Verse number 30,' he replies.

'All right, carry on from there.'

A still uncertain voice begins to speak; it is rather hoarse as it plunges into deep, masculine tones before abruptly slipping back into the shrill voice of a child. Marie listens to this 'breaking' voice:

'*Arcades*, the Arcadians … *cantare periti*, little songs, are easy to recite. *Oh mihi tum quam molliter ossa quiescant …*'

She turns the page; she is using the same book that she herself used in class. She notices a pencilled note in the margin, rather faded and written in a clumsy hand. Leaning over the book she deciphers: 'For me, Nathaniel, the genuineness of my pleasure is the most important of guides.' Opposite verse 38 – of course! She smiles, recalling herself in a tartan dress, reddish hair tied at the nape of the neck with a black ribbon. She remembers this same Marie in a grey suit, eyes sparkling, leaving an auditorium at the Sorbonne, looking at her wrist-watch and making her way towards the Centrale. She remembers her love for Jean, the passionate crushing of fragile bones. Then she sees a Marie who obliterates herself, who disappears, turns into another Marie whose eyes are closed to the world, who only reveres a universe inhabited by those two lively, expressive eyes, that fair, springy hair, those two broad shoulders, those two strong hands; a Marie who is painfully tense, who builds up, constructs, protects.

'*Mecum inter salices lenta sub vite jaceret ...*'

The pupil's voice stops abruptly. Seeing that Marie is far away he looks at the hands, the arms, the shoulders of the young woman, letting his gaze come to rest upon her dress, at the point where her breasts lift the material upwards. Marie intercepts his look and, in a firm voice that is intended to reintroduce a strict working atmosphere, urges her pupil to translate. But since she hasn't been following the text, all she has in her head are the last words she has heard him say.

'Come on, translate! What is the subject of the verb "*jaceret*"?'

The adolescent hesitates; he is at a loss.

'Well? What would have been lying under the flexible vine?'

'The object of my love,' replies the schoolboy, blushing.

As men develop, their veils drop one by one, laying their lives bare; they have so many paths to choose from. Marie is moved as she looks at the child. She'd like to hold out her hand to him, to say something like: 'Don't trust your heart ...'

But the boy's hoarse voice resumes, by turns deep and shrill: '*Serta mihi Phyllis legeret ...*'

When the lesson is over Marie claims some homework from him. 'That essay your school friends did while you were away – I'd like you to do it for me. Bring it with you next Thursday.'

'All right,' the boy says feebly, already seeing his week ruined by the task.

'What was the subject?'

He reels off a sentence in a tone of disgust that amuses

her. She looks at his shoulders, already a man's, at his pale face, at his ink-stained fingers, at his clumsy way of standing – still very much a child's. Again she sees herself, with startling clarity, in her tartan dress.

'Tell me, is it boring for you to have to write that essay?'

'Oh yes!' the child replies openly.

'And do you find Virgil boring, too?'

'No, I don't find Virgil boring.'

'All right, you needn't write the essay, I'll find you another subject. But for the next lesson, I want you to translate the following twenty verses of the tenth Bucolic.'

When the child leaves the apartment Marie half leans over the banisters to watch him go. As happy children do, he skips down the stairs hitting each step in a crazy rhythm, and soon his voice tunes in with his feet in a silly song: 'Knock, knock, who's there? MOSCOW! No ess-ay, only some Vir-gil to translate … Wow, that's a teacher and a half! What a terrific woman! Wom-an, wom-an … Mos-cow what? Mos-n't let her shake me like a plum tree …'

Marie goes back in, laughing at the top of her voice. She's laughing at everything: at the peculiar song, at the child's happiness, at '*jaceret*', at herself.

The moment she's inside the room she hears the phone ring. She listens, replies, and replaces the receiver, her happiness abruptly shattered: Jean will not be home for dinner tonight. She'll spend a long, miserable evening sitting huddled in an armchair, feeling tired and anxious, her features drawn, waiting for him to get back. She'll cry because Jean isn't there, right next to her, because she can neither see his face nor feel the warmth of his body with her hands. How she weeps, secretly, when Jean spends entire evenings with vain, flirtatious girls like Simone and Alice. She weeps the strange, bitter tears of an exhausted woman who is gradually letting herself be worn out by a symbol.

SHE WILL BE ALL ALONE, the whole long evening. Yet she likes solitude, so why is she feeling like this? She will eat in the kitchen, feet on the bar of the stool, knees up to her chin. One plate, and a chunk of bread that she will cut into little pieces with her knife, in the way that she has seen men do on the side of the road. She will make herself some hot coffee, she will read, for a long time, without anything to distract her from her book. She'll spend the entire evening on her own, in a delicious state of solitude.

She looks around her, around Jean and Marie's apartment, letting her gaze wander over the furniture and the belongings. How odd everything seems; has something changed? No, the furniture and belongings have the same familiar, precious look about them, the same halo bestowed upon them by her heart, and her love is exactly as it has always been. Neither the belongings nor the feelings have changed – but they have been confronted.

Resting her hands on her forehead, Marie closes her eyes. How hot it had been! How beautiful the mountain, and the smell of crushed mint beneath their bodies! This desire she felt inside her was so strong, so blissful, so right.

THE ARRIVAL OF THE PUPIL having prevented Marie from finishing the housework, she fills the sink with hot water and begins to wash the dishes.

A few days ago, a young woman in a linen skirt was sitting on a sunny beach. Today, a young woman plunges tanned hands into soapy water, goes down to the cellar to fetch the coal, cleans the floor, peels the vegetables. Marie thinks of other young women she knows and smiles at the astonishment they would feel if they could see her now. What did these other women think of Marie; why does she feel herself to be so different, and why has she never succeeded in really becoming their friend? Perhaps life is simpler if your world is like theirs, confined to choosing wallpaper or sofa covers, to a luxurious home, to the importance of having a maid, to immaculate receptions, to tea parties with friends where a few ideas are exchanged on the latest books. If they have a child, they love it not because it is flesh of their flesh but because it has finally given some point to their existence. They give the impression of being happy or, if they are not, they speak of happiness as an unusable, clearly defined object that need only be discovered and then hung in the apartment like a sprig of mistletoe.

If Marie had a child she would love it with all her flesh and all her heart, but she feels neither regret nor joy at the fact that she does not have one. She doesn't want a child as one wants an ideal, she likes neither luxury nor receptions, she has scarcely any friends, she hates choosing wallpaper, and she does not believe in happiness. Does this mean she loves nothing, awaits nothing?

She has finished her household task and before going into another room to rest and read, she lingers in the kitchen for a while. Sitting at the table, head in hands, she hears the sound of her blood, beating loudly, powerfully, rapidly, at her temples. By separating her arms from her body she can even control the pulsations through that single sensation in her head. These muffled, rhythmical shocks are accompanied by an unusual sound, like a buzzing or a reverberation. She compares it to the sound of insects' wings – smooth, shiny.

What kind of a girl had she been? Very tall and slim, with reddish-blonde hair tied by a black ribbon at the nape of her neck, and two well-shaped breasts under her dress. Sixteen or seventeen years old; beautiful, supple, full of health and happiness; she was drunk with life, and with an overflowing heart.

Are you there, Marie? If only she could never leave me … She is there, right next to me; I can feel her heart beating. She haunts me as if she were waiting to be reborn.

If her friends were there at this moment, and asked her: 'What are you thinking about, Marie?', she couldn't answer: 'I am comparing the sound of my blood to the sound of insects' wings.' She'd smile, and say only: 'Leave me be, I'm asleep.' She'd appear weary, indifferent; she'd turn away to listen once more to the tumultuous pounding of her blood.

Does Marie love nothing, await nothing?

Marie's heart is overflowing with love. Marie awaits Marie.

CHAPTER FOUR

'Isn't monsieur going to Maubeuge this month, Madame?'

'Yes, Germaine, he's going as usual.'

'Shall we take the chance to sort out the wardrobes? If you tidied them, I could clean them and put in new lining paper.'

'Oh no, Germaine, no. Let's leave the wardrobes as they are …'

Marie packed Jean's suitcase as usual, got up early and made his picnic lunch. And as always, when the moment came to say goodbye, she cried on his shoulder because they were going to be separated for three whole days. She went downstairs with him, all the way to the taxi that was waiting outside.

'Goodbye, my dear.'

'Goodbye, Jean, until the day after tomorrow. I'll come and collect you at the station.'

As she went back into the apartment, her shoulders suddenly sagging a little, her head bent forward, it was hard to tell whether the expression on her face was one of sadness or of courage.

She gets up, makes her way to the bedroom. When she emerges a little while later she is wearing an autumn suit. She is lightly made up and her springy hair curls around a tiny beret.

PARIS IS ESPECIALLY BEAUTIFUL in the autumn. Marie loved the streets, the squares, the houses; she was alive to the poetry that the city exudes. Today she instinctively sought out places she hardly ever visited. She had no lunch and by about four o'clock, feeling hungry, she sat down at a pavement café and ordered coffee and a brioche.

From time to time someone shouted: 'Paris Soir, Paris Soir!' Should she buy a newspaper? To find out that a local conflict was in danger of spreading to Europe, to endure hours of wracking fear only to discover the next morning that the London *Times* had declared that the international situation was more stable than it had been a few months earlier, and then to be plunged into anguish yet again because a German ship ... Life goes on, slips through one's fingers. There is fighting in the south, there are arguments in the east, there will be fighting here. People place all their hopes in Russia, and then complain that the country has lapsed into conformity ... People throw themselves into fascism, men fight, thousands of unemployed workers are starving.

So what? Sympathy – sympathy for others? Marie feels elevated, enhanced, by a wild egoism. She thinks: Society? I don't care about society – only the individual interests me. To each his own life.

She is hungry again. She orders a sandwich and bites into it with her mouth wide open, holding the bread with her whole hand. No one looks at her or bothers about her; she feels happy. In this vibrant city, with its noises all around her, she feels completely, delightfully alone. A flower seller passes and holds out a bouquet to her. Oh, not violets, please ...

She stays like this for some time. The night falls softly around her and gradually lights up, becomes striped by neon. She looks at her hands, her arms, her legs, crossed beneath her skirt. She feels young, healthy, strong; rich, tumultuous blood pounds at her temples. Like the sound of insects' wings ...

She gets up, goes inside the cafe and asks the cashier for a token.

'The telephone is at the bottom of the corridor, Mademoiselle.'

Mademoiselle! Marie smiles as she shuts the door of the booth. W, A, G, one, seven, four, two ...

RETURNING TO THE PAVEMENT she paid the bill and continued to wander aimlessly along the boulevards. On this soft September evening, happiness was in the air. Instead of having supper she went into another café and drank a coffee at the counter. All around her she could hear men talking. She had another coffee, looked at the time, tidied her hair.

This time, when she got outside, she took her bearings. She made her way slowly: tall, straight, head held high.

She saw the café from a long way away, at the corner of the two roads, and checked the sign. Going in, she recognised him straight away, and held out her hand. She took him in, all of him: his face, his eyes, his shoulders. The reality of him coincided exactly with her memory.

A waiter came up and stood while Marie decided what to drink.

'A Perrier,' she said, though she never ordered water.

Was she moved, had she lost her nerve, or was it shyness that she felt? Some things in life were important and others were not. And at that moment it really mattered very little whether she was brought tea, water, or vermouth. She pushed the glass away without touching it. Until now they hadn't spoken to each other.

Finally she said, quite simply: 'I could have waited to bump into you by chance, but even if I believe in miracles, I like to connive with them.'

'I was waiting for your phone call ...'

She lit her own cigarette, without asking him for a light. His hand was on the table, and she watched it for a long time. She was not thinking. She was only able to hear, feel and see. She was aware of the slightest sound around her, she smelled the slightest scent in the air. And if she appeared to be letting her gaze wander indifferently round the room, she frequently brought it back to the table. All she was really looking at was the young face opposite her.

He got up, standing aside to let her pass.

'Do you want to walk or would you prefer to take a taxi?'

'Let's walk.'

The darkening streets were almost deserted. They didn't speak. Words would have been a coating on reality, would have forced them into a 'confession'. They were strong enough to look reality in the face; their desire was imperious enough to survive acknowledgement. They wanted to proceed like this towards a precise end, in a spirit of tacit, voluntary agreement. The night was fine, there was joy in the air, and they were moving towards that joy.

Stopping at a door that opened on to a brightly lit corridor, he touched her on the shoulder and said: 'Go on in.'

They went up in a very narrow elevator where there was only room for two bodies face to face. Young maids in canvas pinafores, organdie bows in their hair, bright red lips in inscrutable faces, slip like spirits through the deserted corridors, respecting the anonymity, the secrets of every soul, and folding up quilts with vestal movements. Muffled sounds, orders given in low voices, words that turn into mysteries, doors that shut without a sound. The peace and safety of a temple, with all the solemn, human poetry of a lodging house.

Marie kept quite still and held her breath. He drew her head towards him and they stayed like that for a moment, as if in contemplation. He lifted her up, put her on the bed and gently took off her clothes, as though she were a little girl. She let him do it, helping him by raising her arms and her knees. Soon all she could see were his eyes, close to hers. She wept tears of happiness – a happiness that was suddenly too strong to bear.

COMPLETELY NAKED, Marie gets out of bed and draws the velvet curtains. They close badly, so she reaches across towards the fireplace and fumbles for her brooch, which she attaches to the edge of the two bits of material. Work without witness, a struggle with nature that she presided over without any sense of shame. Returning to bed – victorious or vanquished? – she slips in beside the man who is awaiting her. He has not fallen asleep. Woman, may your happiness endure …

Tender moments in which Marie relishes a face, a forehead, and eyes at once sparkling and soft, so beautiful that she cannot look into them with serenity. Slim, tanned shoulders; long, thin arms; delicate wrists; long hands, like a child's. So very tall, and yet he's scarcely more than an adolescent. She listens, with pride and emotion, to the irregular beating of his heart. She selects a lock of his black, springy hair, pushes it back on his face, liberates it suddenly, and then laughs, because it curls back of its own accord, like a tiny elastic snake. Short hair that she kisses, caresses, spreads out in a fan shape on the pillow and holds up against her own cheek, so that their two faces become confused. 'Through your hair I can see the entire universe …'

And then it's his turn to attend to her, caressing her shoulders, her arms, her hips, discovering absurd, delightful things and looking at her hair: 'You have such beautiful hair ...'

Marie makes a face, like a shy child: 'No, you're so much prettier than me ...'

He raises his eyebrows and says, in deadly earnest: 'I love the colour of your hair.'

Marie sees his face and gestures alter and feels their great, insatiable desire surging up again. Long after the dawn light had dimmed the brightness of the lamps in the room, they had still not given in to sleep. Finally, as the soft autumn sun lit up the windows, they fell asleep peacefully, encircled in each other's arms.

MARIE WAS THE FIRST to awake.

He hadn't moved while they had slept, and when she woke she found herself still in the arms that had fulfilled their task. To Marie, this was a miracle – to find that they were still leaning against one another, her head resting against his male shoulders at the very point where he had placed it before they slept. And she was still full of joy.

Without disengaging herself from the embrace, she raised her head a little so she could look at him. Women like to watch men while they are asleep: it's at such moments that they can give full vent to their tenderness.

He opened his eyes and, tightening his arms around her shoulders, said softly: 'You're there ...'

Her head had fallen back on to his body and they stayed like this. They hadn't turned off the lights in the room and these gave out an unnatural glow that now mingled with and was eclipsed by the daylight. Only from far away did the noise of the busy city reach this quiet street; all was peace, in them and around them.

LEAVING THE BUILDING, they walked without speaking. Strange moments, when they seemed far away from each other whilst possibly thinking the same thoughts.

'Shall I take you to the Métro or to the bus?'

'No, I'll be fine on my own.'

At the first crossroads, they shook hands and separated, with an almost brutal simplicity.

CHAPTER FIVE

INSTEAD OF GOING HOME MARIE continued to walk aimlessly around Paris. Head and heart empty, she lived only in the present, and as she wandered along the streets and boulevards, took in only what opened up before her. At the Faubourg du Temple a man fills his mouth with petrol, sets fire to it and spits out enormous flames. Further on a couple are singing a desperate, nostalgic song. A man passes her dressed in an old raincoat and a Basque beret; he is pushing a pram containing a sleeping child, and two other children walk either side of him, hanging on to his arms. For a long time, Marie follows the same route as this man.

She sits down in a square and talks to three little girls who are playing ball. At the place de l'Opéra, she leans on the railings of the entrance to the Métro and looks at the handsome dragoon on horseback. She goes down the steps, enters a compartment and gets off at a station whose name takes her fancy.

Time passed quickly. Behind windows, in brightly lit cafés, people were sitting down to eat. Marie walked into one; it was the first time in her life that she had ever eaten alone in a restaurant. She ordered a meal and some burgundy. Her cheeks reddened and as a gentle warmth enveloped her she began to emerge from her state of semi-consciousness. Her heart re-awoke and filled with all the memories of the previous night. She remembered those two arms around her with special sweetness. She recaptured, intact and perfect, the memory of a precise moment – when, still beside himself, he had let his head fall back on to her body. She'd tightened her arms around him and said, in a barely audible voice, not knowing whether he could hear her or not, as if it were a terrible thing that you are not allowed to say but that is so powerful it forces its way through your lips: 'I love you.' Again she rediscovered the warmth of that young body and saw his tender eyes so close to hers. Although her hands were still, one lying in her lap and the other on the tablecloth, she felt that if she raised them and stretched them out a little in front of her she would feel, softly but precisely, the outline of his slender shoulders.

Rising up, taking sudden shape with these memories, a whole new world was born.

She remained still, her eyes vague. Now she was seeing him a little while before he'd left the room. He had talked about the holidays being over, of a provincial university that he would be leaving for very soon. He'd given her a new telephone number. It was then that she had come out with a halting sentence which betrayed her embarrassment that she alone, yet again, held their future in her hands. He'd shrugged his shoulders: 'It looks as if I have more freedom than you, then.' As they were leaving the room he had drawn her close to kiss her and held her tightly, gently, to his chest before opening the door: 'After you.' It was as if an iron curtain had been pulled behind them. A few moments later they had their simple, brusque separation at the crossroads in the rue de Chateaudun.

So she was now in possession of another four figures preceded by a name – the name of a town five hundred kilometres away. She felt that he was going to leave very soon, tomorrow or even today, perhaps at this very moment. She saw a railway station, raised hands, a train setting off. She had already been through tender farewells with Jean, and now there was this short, brusque departure at the crossroads in the rue de Chateaudun. She sat there, without moving, haunted by his image, feeling three times wounded. To involve yourself in more than one love is also to involve yourself in more than one heartbreak – and, more than likely, in regular periods of loneliness, too. Jean she would find again tomorrow, but what about this young creature of the previous night, this wild passion with no definite future?

Her throat tightened and tears came to her eyes. She got up to leave, to rediscover the noise, the movement, the colours of the street, though she was hesitant about confronting this vibrant scene on her own. She began to walk, as if sleepwalking, moving onwards in a coloured haze. She went into the café she'd been in the previous evening. Behind the counter the cashier was making the same gestures with the same tired smile. Once again Marie drank the bitter coffee. Up at the bar, men and women were quickly downing their drinks, then leaving and making way for others – new faces which gave Marie a sense of herself, a deprived feeling of solitude. She would have liked to have followed these men and women without them knowing it, to find out whether their happiness and their pain were similar in any way.

She walked for a long time, following deserted roads, crossing busy boulevards, then along dark streets again. She walked like this, with her big, calm, springy step, all the way to where she lived, without a single detour.

She went to the bedroom straight away, stretching out without fear on the cold, empty bed.

In her thoughts she saw a train, deep in the night, making its way through the countryside. A very young man was lying on one of the wooden benches, content with the thought that his youth was being taken towards an unknown life. She saw another man, rather older than the first, in a hotel bedroom in a northern town. He was stretching out his arms, all relaxed, glad to have a bed to himself.

Marie was experiencing a deep sense of pain. Confronting it objectively, she decided that it had its proper place in the order of things. Stretching her tired limbs out across the bed, she revelled in the exhaustion of her back and legs, in this heavy appeasement of her senses.

It was very late; the dawn light was already shining when Marie fell asleep. With her strong face, and her big body moulded by the sheets, she did not look like a woman who'd just been left by a man. She looked more like an ancient, masculine form, a young creature who had gone to sleep, body appeased, and whose sleep had been inhabited by big, warlike dreams.

CHAPTER SIX

THE GARE DU NORD is dark, dirty, in a state of decay, and new arrivals bring back memories of the depressing landscapes they've just passed through. In the third-class trains, the journey from the frontier is unbearable. From time to time a sports team or a group of Catholics will alight from those trains with a flourish – they'll cross the station with flags unfolded and greet Paris with a tired, noisy rendering of the Belgian national anthem. On the platforms, people waiting for arrivals or departures speak in the heavy tones of Flanders or with a Walloon drawl.

The Maubeuge train was late; Marie was sitting in the station buffet watching the platform. She saw some red lights but no, it wasn't the train. She got up to look at the board announcing delays – the number of minutes had increased by fifteen. She continued to wait until she saw a crowd of people pressing through the barrier. She went up to him immediately.

'You're not too tired, Jean? Here, give me your case.'

She walked very close to him, slipping an arm through his. How pleased she was that he was back, but how tired he looked, and how lined his brow … She thought his face was dirty but it was stubble darkening his chin and his cheeks. Even though he shaved every day, he always had a dark shadow.

Marie stood opposite Jean in the bus.

'What did you do in the evenings, darling?'

She replied, off the top of her head: 'Oh, I read, I prepared my teaching. What was the weather like up there?'

'Rain as usual. There haven't been any important letters, then?'

'No, you'll see. Do you think your trip went well? Are sales good?'

'Hardly – the recession goes on and on. At the moment it's best if I'm on the spot.'

In the early days of their marriage Jean had accepted a job as an engineer with a firm in Maubeuge, his home town, and he feared that they would have to leave the Paris that Marie loved so much, and where he had just spent five years of student life. But the firm had opened an office in Paris, which meant that Jean could live there; he only had to spend short periods in Maubeuge in order to deal with the technical side of his work.

'I don't understand,' Marie said. 'If sales are down, why does your presence become more and more necessary?'

'They're talking about closing the Paris office,' he replied softly.

Marie said nothing. In her mind's eye she remembered the few days they had spent at Maubeuge a month after their marriage: the narrow, colourless town, the family circle, the big dark house behind the factory. That would be terrible, she thought. Suddenly, too, she saw the number of kilometres increasing again, changing from five to seven hundred. 'That would be terrible!' she said out loud.

'If it came to that, it would probably only last a few months. And anyway, if it would be too painful for you, I could live there alone and you could stay here.'

'Oh no,' she replied without hesitation.

'Let's not think about it,' he said. 'Nothing is definite yet.'

They went home and sat down to eat. She had prepared a soup that she'd left to cook on the side of the stove, and served it up piping hot. She felt happy to be serving it up to Jean piping hot, happy too that he was sitting at table, in his place, next to her.

'I am very happy,' she said, 'now that you are here with me.'

She looked at him and saw again the beard, the lines on his brow and other lighter ones around his eyes.

'Have you been working too hard? You look so tired.'

'I look tired?'

He got up and turned towards the mirror. 'What do you mean – I look fine!'

He was right: that was just the way he looked. His face was neither tired nor old; it was only thirty-two.

'Did you see your mother?' he asked.

'No, I spent an afternoon with her last week.'

'Usually you can't go two days without running over to her to find out whether she has any problems!'

'I preferred to be alone.'

THERE WAS A KIND OF CONFIDENCE in Marie's voice, in her gestures, in the way she held her head. Jean took in the brightness of her gaze, the darkness of her eyes. How beautiful she is, he thought.

'Have you seen Claudine?' he asked. 'She must have got back from holiday several days ago.'

Her sister Claudine. Marie and Claudine shared an intimacy that made them more like friends than sisters. She had last written to her when they were on holiday, three days before her encounter, and in the days that followed she'd scarcely thought about her at all. For the last three days she had forgotten Claudine.

Although Claudine was the elder sister she had always seemed the more childish. When they were little it was Claudine who smeared her exercise books with ink and chocolate. She was smaller than Marie, with small features and light, mousy hair. Their mother used to call them, jokingly, 'my little brunette and my big redhead' – it used slightly to annoy Marie that she should exaggerate the colour of her hair in this way. As an adolescent Claudine liked the same books as Marie, quoted the same passages, had the same desires, the same enthusiasms, the same dislikes. And Marie admired her sister, thought her destined for a full, dramatic life. She didn't know then that whereas all those things were deeply rooted in her, for Claudine they were only superficial passions, as if she were acting. When Claudine talked, she dazzled their friends, but she was only parroting the words of Marie – who was taciturn and inscrutable, confiding in no one but her sister. Marie thought Claudine was the only person who could understand her; she spoke to her without realising that she was speaking to her own image.

At the age of eighteen Claudine gave herself to a student, just because he was the first man to make a pass at her. Afterwards, in a state of shock after a visit to an obliging doctor, she had taken refuge in her sister's arms. Marie could still see the bedroom they shared as girls: the lamp they had to cover so that no one would see it was still on, and Claudine's childish fears, which she continually tried to allay. She had put her hand rather firmly on Claudine's mouth to stop her calling out to their mother; later she'd hidden the blood-soaked sheets.

Claudine blocks out the episode and begins to play around again, carelessly abandoning herself to fortune. She knows nothing of love, of joy or of sorrow, but she speaks of them in big, extravagant words that lose meaning on her lips. At twenty-three, she marries a man of forty, because 'everything is hopeless anyway', because 'I'm fed up' and because she wants to be free. Free to do what, for God's sake? 'Hopeless', 'fed up': Marie has a horror of such words. Can Claudine really be the kind of person who uses them, one of those desperate little people who says that 'nothing is worth the effort'? Marie agonises over this: how she would like to save her!

Claudine travels a lot, usually without her husband. Her nights are spent without love, joy or danger: she goes no further than bold embraces, not performing any act that might commit her: 'It's much easier that way.' She tells Marie everything, not knowing whether she should laugh or cry at her own behaviour. Finally, laughing and with a great declamatory gesture, she announces, by way of explanation: 'Whenever I sleep alone, I'm afraid I will die.'

It had been a long time since Marie stopped admiring Claudine, but she never stopped loving her – with a deep, almost painful love. She went on talking to her intimately, involving her in the smallest details of her life, not because she needed to confide in her, but as if in homage to someone she had once admired, to an odd kind of love which persisted in spite of everything, which nothing would ever diminish.

And now there is this completely new, beautiful love inside her, this secret, so full of light, that she does not want to share with Claudine. For the first time, her love for Claudine is an embarrassment.

MARIE HADN'T ANSWERED Jean's question. It didn't surprise him: he knew that Claudine was a disappointment to Marie, that this grieved her, and that she often preferred not to talk about it.

They went into their bedroom. Marie got into bed first and as she watched him take off his clothes she had an inkling that his body would smell slightly of sweat. 'You ought to wash,' she said, 'after that train journey.'

'Wash?' he said, annoyed. 'OK, if you want.'

But what Marie had feared did not take place. Almost as soon as he was in bed Jean went to sleep. Without waking him, she slipped her arms around him, rediscovering his heat, his panting chest, his heavy shoulders. She was sorry now that she could smell only soap and water on his skin; she had feared the smell of him not because it was unpleasant, but because it was his. And now she craved that smell, because she would have loved it as a mother loves the smell of her child.

CHAPTER SEVEN

'YES, CLAUDINE, OF COURSE ...'
Thinking about her sister the next morning Marie was almost happy to feel herself moved: she still loved her after all. Germaine was coming in today so she could leave the housekeeping to her until midday. She would go and see her sister.

SHE RANG THE BELL, waited a long time. She heard slippers shuffling along the floor of the corridor, then saw her: she looked thinner, in spite of her tan.

Claudine had only just got out of bed and was feeling cold: it was a shame, she said, that they hadn't yet turned on the central heating. She'd make an instant fire in the grate that lined the fireplace. She went to the kitchen to look for wood and coal.

She scattered the wood clumsily as she returned, and dropped some of the coal. When the fire failed to take because she didn't wait for the wood to light, she gave up completely and sat down, sighing.

'Are you really cold?' Marie asked.

'Yes, but it's too boring to light the fire,' she replied, with a child's temper.

'It's too boring because you don't know how to do it,' Marie said.

She laid out a newspaper on the floor, emptied the contents of the grate and started all over again. She thought to herself: Or perhaps it's more that she doesn't know how to do it because she finds it so boring …

Yes, that's it: Claudine is bad at lighting fires because Claudine doesn't like wood, or coal, or the smell of the fire which is beginning to take. For Claudine, it is the same for all work of this kind: whether she's scrubbing a floor, or cleaning a pan, or polishing an object, she does it clumsily.

By contrast, Marie accomplishes such tasks neatly: in her apartment the coal drawers are always full and everything sparkles. And yet, Marie reflects, there's no value whatsoever in this – it's simply that she likes undertaking this kind of task. When she comes up from the cellar, she enjoys the weight of the full coal-buckets, even though they seem heavier with every step. She has always felt affection for simple things that have their own particular smell, their own particular roughness, and she's always known how to handle them. Without fear or hesitation her hands plunge into dead fires or into soapy water, they rub the rust off a piece of metal and grease it, spread polish, and, after a meal, sweep the scraps from a table in one great circular movement. It's a perfect harmony, a mutual understanding between the palms of her hands and the objects they touch. She reflects that however completely people might fulfil themselves in other spheres, if they don't possess this understanding between their hands and material objects, they can never have more than an incomplete understanding of the world. It is this mutual understanding that makes movements succeed.

She likes hands that understand what inanimate objects are saying, and that know how to speak to living things, too. She likes hands that rest on a shoulder and grasp it, hands that suggest all the richness of the heart more effectively than any verbal expressions of love, simply by holding them around a face.

CLAUDINE HAD BEEN WATCHING Marie as she worked away. When her sister had rung the bell, she hadn't been able to find her dressing gown and had thrown on a beige canvas apron instead, attaching it at the waist with a piece of cord. She hadn't used a comb, and with her short, dull brown hair all over her forehead, her thin face and her dark unmade-up skin, she looked like a sickly little peasant.

She talked of holidays that had gone wrong, she yawned, she complained. Marie wished she'd stop: with every word something in her wavered, with every word her love for Claudine was in danger of dying. And when she herself wanted to talk, she lied a little with each sentence she uttered, because there was this great new thing that she was concealing like a treasure, and which meant that nothing else she might say had any reality. She wanted to leave; and at other moments she wanted to take this grubby little body into her arms and say: 'Come on, get dressed quickly, and come with me to look at things.' Look at what? She could only have said the streets, the Seine, the sun, men, women, the buses. And to Claudine, that answer would have seemed stupid.

As she left, she embraced her sister a little too tightly and told her that she would phone soon.

CLAUDINE LIVED FAR FROM the Right Bank, and the bus that took Marie towards the centre of town travelled the length of the rue de Rennes, crossed the boulevard St Germain and then stopped. A public clock was showing only a quarter to twelve, and since it was warm Marie left the bus and went to sit on one of the benches in front of the church. A fine end of September sun was flooding the terrace of the celebrated café and almost the whole width of the street, lighting up the blue awning of a bookshop. Marie thought of Claudine and how she had left her, with her skinny face, her worn-out old slippers, her makeshift apron. She'd probably be wandering about the apartment now, not doing anything at all; or she might have gone back to bed after her sister had left. Marie's heart sank. She ought to have taken her by force, made her call her husband and suggest they both come to lunch.

If she'd done that Claudine would be with her; Claudine would be talking. And Marie would no longer be alone: she would not be looking at the buses shining in the sun before making their darker passage into the rue Bonaparte. This notion quickly put paid to her remorse. She declared: 'I am going through a period of self-absorption; it will pass.'

Self-absorption, yes, that was it, but self-absorption of a rather particular kind. It seemed to her that in the last few years she had held in her hands a series of reins, each of which was tied only to the people who inhabited her own life. 'Jean, our love will last forever ...' 'I tell you, it is rare indeed that people love each other as much as Marie and I do ...' 'Jean, about our love ...' 'Yes, darling, about our love ...' 'Jean, you're not going out all alone to this party after all, are you, without me?' 'But no, my sweet, it would never have entered my head to go without you.' 'Claudine, I've just discovered a little poem by Louise Labé, as I was thumbing through a rare edition in a bookshop ... I've learnt it by heart, it's wonderful – listen!' 'Wonderful ...' 'And straight away, Claudine, I looked forward to telling you about it – I'm going to dictate it to you.' 'Oh yes, Marie, please let me hear it!'

So it was that whole minutes, hours, years passed by – all full, fine and perfect in their way, but essentially artificial, for if Marie were not in charge of them, these moments would not exist; she alone constructs them, with her heart, her flesh, her personal desires. This was her only faith, and it shone as brightly as the reins she held in her hands.

One summer morning, Marie turned her head and looked behind her. She let go of the reins, and her newly liberated hands began to search for something in the past.

Sitting on a bench in front of Saint-Germain-des-Prés, she stared without seeing it at the corner of the rue de Rennes and the rue de l'Abbaye. Again an image haunted her: of a tall girl with reddish hair adjusting a lampshade so that the light did not disturb Claudine's sleep, then sitting down at a table with her hands on her forehead, heart pounding in great regular beats, and reading Nietzsche's *Beyond Good and Evil*.

She recalled the starched cotton collar that she sometimes wore on top of her dress: the neck was fastened with a false-stitched linen border that kept coming apart, so you had to push it back against the material with your thumb or index finger. Fully recapturing the irritation she had felt in her fingers filled her with a sense of joy and triumph.

Marie re-awoke to the objects, the sounds and the place where she was sitting to see a man on the pavement terrace opposite; he was turning towards her and waving hello. Recognising him as Marius Denis, she didn't move. He called to her again and finally got up and joined her.

'What are you doing sitting on that bench, Marie?'

'I'm rushing home,' she replied, laughing.

'You'd do better to come and have a drink with me. Will you?'

'It's just as nice here as it is opposite.'

A little put out, he sat by her on the bench. Marius Denis had desired Marie because he desired women. Perhaps he desired them quickly and briefly because, as a good psychologist, he always managed to find the particular language that would make them yield to him. In this context, every time he had spoken to Marie she had heard him with good grace and an attentive air; it was he who awaited a reaction that did not come. An intelligent man, he had understood that Marie was not really listening to him, that she remained distant, as if enclosed in some private world. She rarely responded to what he said, and even then never with a complete sentence. Sometimes she would wake up at a word that he had just said, bestowing upon him a sharp look as if she were following a definite path, but then, as if satisfied, her eyes would soften and she would retreat to her distance. He found these brief awakenings of her gaze even more disconcerting than the long periods of dormancy: when her eyes were sleepy there was just a chance she would give in, but when they were clear and bright she would not. A woman who was faithful to her husband and who would not give herself to anyone was rare enough; a woman who would not give herself to him, that was unthinkable. It followed that Marius's desire for Marie grew ever more acute, but he spoke to her only of generalities.

They had been at the Sorbonne together: he was involved in many kinds of literary activity so they had several areas of mutual interest. From time to time he slipped in to their conversation an ambiguous, almost bitter phrase, as if to convey to her that if he no longer insisted, everything would continue to depend upon her alone.

'Did you have a good holiday?' he asked tritely.

'Not bad.'

After a while, as if realising she had forgotten something, she added: 'What about you, Denis?'

She called him Denis. She'd said to him one day: 'I don't like calling people by their surname, apart from you: "Marius" is rather ridiculous, whereas your surname makes a good first name.' He'd recalled exactly what she said; it was unusual for Marie to utter a sentence like that, one of the rare occasions when she'd said something that related directly to him.

He replied: 'I couldn't afford a big trip so I just went to the Touraine. I've been back in Paris three weeks, I'm working on my new magazine.'

After a few moments he added: 'I've been thinking about you a lot.'

'How can I be of use to you?' she asked coolly.

He had a sudden urge to hit her. Instead, he decided to respond as if his last sentence bore some relation to the one before it.

'You might be of use to me at the magazine. I thought you might be interested in collaborating with me on it some time. You'd need to know what it's all about, you'd have to come to the office so that we could discuss it. If I asked you to come to my place you would refuse, as you always have done.'

'That's because you've always asked me to come for no particular reason, the very day after we've just met and chatted away for as long as we've wanted … And then I probably had other things to do, other people to see.'

Why not call her bluff, he thought? 'You'll come, then? Today at half-past two?'

'I'll be at your place at half-past two.'

She got up and stretched out her hand. He watched her as she walked away, admiring her easy stride and her hair shining in the sun – hair that no hat concealed and no hair-style kept in check.

Was it possible that today was his lucky day, when he would find an intelligent collaborator as well as the woman he had desired for so long?

Marie, meanwhile, had gone into a bookshop to browse through his magazine. She'd found it to be feminine and fashionable, and wondered what kind of collaboration Denis could possibly have in mind for her.

AT HALF-PAST TWO MARIE entered a building in the rue Marguerin, pushed open the door of the office and asked for Marius Denis. As she waited, she breathed in the exciting smell of ink and new paper. She imagined the back rooms where the magazine was printed, where the smell must be even stronger; she'd have liked to visit them.

But Denis arrived, and said: 'Let's go up to my apartment, it's more comfortable there.'

Not wanting to annoy him she followed, somewhat reluctantly, towards the elevator.

The apartment was small, with only one room; the door opened directly on to a kind of studio furnished with couches, armchairs and shelves full of books. Marie took everything in – the closed curtains, the dim light from a single small lampstand, and the table adorned by two glasses, a cocktail shaker and a plate of biscuits – and grasped the situation immediately.

Feeling distinctly uneasy, she sat down on the sofa in the place indicated by Denis. Her unease was born not of fear – she wasn't at all apprehensive – but of repulsion. He does all these preparations to make women feel more relaxed, she said to herself. It was a kind of trap. And women fell into it because they were giving themselves not to the man who was there with them, to that man rather than to another, but to someone who was so effaced by the darkness of the room that he became almost anonymous; they were yielding not to a man but to an ambience – the dim light, the cushions, the closed curtains, the smell of the wine. The next day they could appease their consciences by saying quietly: 'It was all because of the ambience.'

Marie remained seated, knees together, hands clasped, her whole body filled with physical repugnance. Denis was talking banalities, such as things that had happened to him on holiday. This went on for several minutes whilst he moved closer and closer. Finally he leaned over her handbag, as if to admire it. Marie realised he thought that when he raised his head he could kiss her. She said nothing, but began to laugh without letting him see. She allowed him to place the bag on her lap but immediately took hold of her glass and raised it to her lips, concealing her smile and protecting her mouth at the same time. He stayed where he was, silent, his hand on her knee.

She no longer felt a sense of unease, nor did she want to laugh; she was now profoundly annoyed by the whole scene. She said drily: 'Well now, Denis, what about this magazine?'

He explained that he had launched it for commercial reasons, with a view to being able to spend time on more important work without having to worry so much about money. But now that the new magazine had 'taken off' he thought that he could try to make it appeal to a more intellectual readership whilst preserving its popular nature. He would write some pieces of literary criticism, and Marie a column on philosophy.

'That would be it,' he said. 'You'd be the one who'd give the magazine a bit of class. But remember, I want your articles to make an impression but they must also be accessible to the people who buy it.'

The whole chaotic atmosphere had reduced Marie to a state of extreme irritation; she was in no mood to be compliant. The silent anger that had been rising up in her ever since she had come into the apartment suddenly exploded.

'Listen, Denis, if what you want from me is ten pages on the Critique of Pure Reason, that's fine. And if you want me to help you draft recipes for Veal Marengo, Kromesky Chicken or whatever, that's fine, too, even if I have to make them up. But if you want me to take two spoonfuls of Spinoza, one of Plato, three grams of Bergson, and bind the mixture with a digestive sauce that will suit these ladies' stomachs, that's not on at all. I am quite simply not cut out for that kind of work …'

Marie carried on in the same vein. He had never heard her talk for so long, in such a strong, furious voice. So taken was he by her animated gestures, her nervous hands and her eyes, which had finally come to life – albeit accusingly – for a full few minutes, that he quite forgot to answer back.

When she had finished Denis was in a state of shock, not knowing what to say but wanting to be friendly. He went up to the table and filled her glass. 'What do you think of this drink?'

'It's a little sweet. You ought to have put in less port and more gin,' she said, in a voice still loaded with anger.

Obediently, he poured half the contents away and added more gin. 'You haven't said anything about the apartment,' he said, after a few moments of silence. 'It's just been redesigned, I'd like to know what you think.'

'It's probably very nice, but you can't see the colours with that useless little lamp,' she replied.

And looking at the closed curtains she asked: 'Is that a false window?'

He turned out the lamp and opened the curtains. The room was flooded with light, so sudden and so strong that they blinked.

She got up and stood in the middle of the room. 'If it had been like this when I arrived, things might have turned out differently, in every respect,' she said, giving him a hard look.

After the attitude she had just shown, and the sentence she had just uttered, Denis had only two possible options: to take her by the shoulders and throw her out, or to make love to her. Realising this, Marie felt responsible for the situation, and waited with some concern to see what he would do. Instead of being cross he looked at her and said: 'Do you always reveal yourself like this, Marie, so dramatically?'

She felt sad, her anger suddenly deflated. 'Reveal myself ... reveal myself?' she repeated softly, as though to herself.

'You ought to speak out more often, Marie, to open up a bit. You should speak to other people more often, you'd do them good.'

His voice was guarded, and had taken on an imploring note. Marie looked at him with a tenderness touched with pity – at his hands and his hair, at his weak forehead and his sad, shallow eyes. This was a man she would never love.

Outside, she thought: Poor Denis, he's only a little boy, really, but at a deeper level continued to be angry and repelled. She was hot – she hadn't taken her coat off even for a moment – and she was still nauseated by the taste of the cocktail. She was stifling, she needed air. She passed Alésia Métro and made her way on foot up the avenue d'Orléans.

At a crossroads she was attracted by the sight of a neighbourhood fête. It was like a little funfair – you didn't often see them in Paris.

She stopped in front of a large merry-go-round of the roller-coaster type, a vast multi-coloured moving machine supervised by a tall young man wearing a navy-blue pea-jacket; his cap was set sideways on his fair hair. For the moment he had no customers, but it didn't seem to worry him. As he leaned against the picture that concealed the rotating wheel, he had the air of an indifferent but all-powerful master, like a god who might enjoy watching his world revolve whilst awaiting the moment when he feels the urge to fill it with people. He stopped the merry-go-round then started it again – out of habit, or perhaps out of caprice. Then he spotted Marie standing nearby, watching him. He cried out: 'Hey, big beauty, come over here!'

Smiling, she jumped on to the floor, which was already vibrating, all ready to go. The man held out his hands, then seized her just as the merry-go-round was starting, and sat her on a horse. 'I'm putting you on the biggest one – for the same price as the smallest!'

He rode pillion behind her, taking hold of her wrists and reaching his arms over hers in a double cross. Without holding on to anything, they were carried faster and faster, around and around. He propelled her along from his torso and arms, transmitting to her chest a long, deep, come-and-go routine – depending on whether the merry-go-round was moving up or down. 'It's like waves in the sea!' he said. 'A very stormy sea!' she retorted.

The phrase pleased him so much that he began to sing it, to the restrained, cracked melody of the carousel. They were now going at maximum speed, and when they were on the down-ward slope, Marie's hair streamed behind her. The man was no longer singing, but breathing like a siren, softly going up, briskly going down; on the flat bits he held on to her more tightly.

When the machine had slowed down and he'd pulled up the brake, Marie held out her thirty sous, the advertised price for the ride. He hesitated, wanting to refuse but not daring to do so. He found a solution: he accepted the money and said: 'Shall we go and have a drink in the café opposite, so I can keep an eye on my stand?'

'Yes!' she said, delighted.

They went into the bar. The man was so tall that in order to lean his elbow on the counter he had to stand in an unnatural position, but he managed it gracefully, his thighs in an elegant curve.

Looking at Marie, he said: 'I can't make it out, it's very unusual: a young woman like you in such a nicely cut coat, so well turned out and so smart – all alone at a fair, without even a hat on ...'

Marie smiled and shrugged her shoulders. She looked across at the merry-go-round and said, as if by way of explanation: 'They're wonderful, fairs.'

'They're not bad,' he conceded.

They talked for a while, about this and that, and, when they'd finished their coffees, left the café.

They shook hands and he said: 'It's funny – you meet someone, you become pals, then you say goodbye ...'

'Yes, it's funny,' she said.

He returned to his merry-go-round and Marie went on her way.

The machine was moving gently. The man sat side-saddle on a horse, opposite to the movement of the circuit, so that he could watch Marie walk away. A few metres on, she turned back towards him and raised her hand; he took off his cap and held it at arm's length in a motionless farewell, observing her with a solemn smile. She saw him for a few seconds only, before the roundabout took this god to the other side of the world.

BACK HOME MARIE FOUND the kitchen in a state of disarray; she'd left straight after lunch without having time to do anything. All that to arrive at the rue Marguerin on the dot, all because of that idiot Denis! She put some water on to boil, tidied up the room, and then paused, her mind going back to the merry-go-round, singing as the man had done, with the words they'd made up. When the water was hot she washed the dishes and put them away. The stove had got spattered as she'd prepared lunch, so she wiped it, ran an emery cloth over it, spread it with a steel-coloured paste and began to scrub it, happily, until the cast iron shone, like a mirror.

CHAPTER EIGHT

IT WAS A FINE OCTOBER, with steady temperatures, every day lit by a pale sun. As the trees of Paris gently shed their leaves, the air filled with a smooth, peaceful sense of mortality.

Marie felt neither enthusiasm, hatred, distress or even indifference, but a kind of wild peace. If she had any desire at all, it was to be a man walking along a road, sleeping and eating on the hoof, sitting on a pile of stones and cutting up his bread with a knife. If she experienced any happiness, it was the strange, hard pleasure of availability. She walked with a steady step, her eyes clear, her head unusually high. The season of the year was dying too gently for the season of her heart which, in the remembrance of a single night, was struck by a flash – a crude, almost cold clarity.

Marie had hardly seen Claudine, and even then it was usually by chance, at a gathering of friends. She had hardly spoken to her, not wanting to see those distressed, abandoned looks that Claudine bestowed on her.

From the outside it looked as if nothing had changed between Jean and Marie. Then one evening, Jean expressed a desire to go to a cinema to see a new Russian film that everyone was talking about. Marie was not drawn to the idea, and said so. Jean seemed surprised and upset by her refusal, but Marie added: 'But you could go on your own – why don't you?'

He was at first astonished, then delighted. He ate his supper fast and after he'd left she heard him whistling away on the stairway – something he hardly ever did. She told herself that Simone and Alice would be at the cinema and that he would come home very late. He hadn't even bothered to finish his pudding; his plate was still half full.

She took all this in without feeling unhappy about it; it only proved what she already knew.

When he came home he found her in bed. Opening her eyes, she said unreproachfully: 'How late you are.'

'I stayed on to have a chat with Alice.'

He was right next to her, and she could see a light-red mark on his cheek, just by his mouth.

'Go and wipe your mouth,' she said.

He went up to the mirror then came towards her. He thought she was going to issue her usual little series of rebukes, or to say how sad she felt, and he wanted to lean over her, kiss her and say, as he always did, that these encounters meant nothing, that the love they shared was unshakeable.

But he could tell from her face that she had gone back to sleep. Her skin seemed paler and her beautiful hair, spread out in curls on the pillow, looked like a shining helmet. That nervous tension in her mouth, which was always there even when she was asleep, had gone, and her breathing was slow, barely perceptible, showing no sign of sadness or precipitation. She was lying on her back with her wrists chastely crossed on her breast, just as she used to when she was fifteen.

When Jean came home late, however deeply asleep Marie was, she would move at the touch of his body when he slipped in beside her; instinctively, she would stretch out her arm and fling it over his chest, in a gesture of protectiveness. Today, in her virginal sleep, she stayed dead to the world.

CHAPTER NINE

A T THE BEGINNING of November Jean left for Maubeuge again. Marie was ready early, and went with him on the bus to the station. A few minutes later she once more found herself staying behind on the platform as the train pulled out.

Nine o'clock on a cold morning, and Paris is bustling. Soon the clouds might disperse, and by midday the air might recapture a degree of warmth, but now Marie walks as rapidly as she can in the increasingly bitter air of the wide Neuilly avenues.

Set amongst the big *hôtels particuliers* is a more modest house, almost hidden by the trees of the neighbouring garden, which extend right along its façade. The impression is not that this park-like garden has strayed on to someone else's property: the smaller building looks as if it's been wedged into someone else's territory.

The narrow path leading to the house looks like a right of way. Marie has walked up it and pulled shut the low gate behind her; she is so accustomed to the noise it makes that she does not hear it. The path lengthens narrowly between two hedges of high shrubs, then widens out towards the left into a small garden which opens out in front of the house. This is where Claudine and Marie played when they were children.

The front door is hardly ever locked. Marie doesn't ring the bell but before lifting the latch she knocks a few times on the wood, quickly, according to a familiar pattern: whether they hear her or not, she has always done this to announce her presence.

In the corridor she walks quickly on – she knows that at this hour her parents will be taking their breakfast in the big glazed kitchen. They are sitting next to each other (when he was alive, her maternal grandfather sat opposite them, with Claudine at one end of the table and Marie at the other) and the maid is near the stove, busy with something or other: she doesn't leave the room because she knows she isn't disturbing them.

'Marie? Hello, darling!'

'Marie, how early you are! You've never turned up so early before!'

'I've just put Jean on the train to Maubeuge.'

'So you've come home to Mum and Dad to seek consolation ...'

'Would you like a cup of cocoa?'

Hot-water chocolate, since Marie's father does not like milk. She delights in the slightly insipid liquid, and the intense memories it revives.

Marie looks at her mother: at this hour she hasn't finished dressing, and her hair, which is still brown, is covered with a hairnet that is supposed to keep her waves in place during the night. She puts a hand up to her absurd-looking hair and apologises with the confused, almost girlish smile that she adopts when talking about herself – always a source of amusement to both husband and daughter. Marie's eyes meet her father's and they laugh; then they both turn towards the woman whose hair is not done and regard her tenderly. Marie says warmly: 'It makes me so happy to see you like that!'

Her father gets up; it's time for him to go to the office.

Marie stays behind with her mother. Even though she never goes more than two weeks without coming back to this house, today it seems as though she's been away for several years; that's what gives her an expression that is both moved and inquisitive. She reaches out fondly to every object, every movement, every word, as if seeking some kind of forgiveness.

She says: 'Have you seen Madame Palafroid recently, Mother?'

Her mother has always made a mess of pronouncing this impossible name and Marie awaits her reply anxiously.

'Yes, I have – Madame Palefroid is very well.'

Marie seizes upon the word 'Palefroid', savouring the 'e' as if it were a precious object.

She gets up and, standing next to the table, looks out of the window. From here you could see the little garden but not the path. She remembers herself and Claudine sitting at the table, heads bent over their big grey cloth-covered exercise books. Hearing someone on the path, they looked at each other and cried out: 'A visitor!' Then, disappointed: 'It's the baker ...'

Marie summons up and recalls all the sounds, the smells, the sights of this garden, and abandons herself to them.

The maid, José, has just come up from the cellar with a basketful of vegetables; she then disappears again to tidy the bedrooms. Marie's mother empties the vegetables on to the table and begins to scrape them. Marie finds a small kitchen knife in the drawer of the dresser and helps her. The two women do not speak: between them there is a peaceful silence inhabited only by the sound of the knives scraping the tough skin of the carrots. So as not to lose a second of her daughter's presence, the mother has postponed the completion of her toilette: she has put on an apron over her morning dress and she is still wearing that odd little hairnet. The faces of both women are at peace.

No more knife noises; the vegetables are scraped. From time to time a drop of water falls from the tap and, without making a sound, plops on to a small dishcloth in the sink. The silence is perfect, ineffable. Leaning over to her mother Marie puts her arm round her waist, pulls her towards her and says quietly: 'On Thursday mornings we used to go to the market together ...'

'Yes, and you always made for the spot where there were the most bits and pieces ... you'd ask me to buy you a heap of old rags ...'

It's not hard to get a mother to talk about the past. As Marie's mother talks and tells stories, she recreates in her heart the little girl that Marie used to be. Looking at this young woman now in her arms, she speaks of a Marie who was still rich in many different kinds of love, who had not yet been overtaken by a single love. Marie lets her go on: she cannot tell her mother that she no longer needs help from memories. She lets her head fall on to the maternal shoulder and rests it there, offering up that instant to her mother alone. A long, miraculous moment in which Marie gives herself back to her mother.

CHAPTER TEN

MARIE HAS JUST LEFT her parents' house, and the wide streets are already less cold. It's not yet midday, but the temperature seems to improve as she approaches the centre of the city. The avenue des Ternes, Beaujon Hospital and Saint-Philippe-du-Roule are cloudy and it is still dull when she reaches the Madeleine and the Opéra. But when she leaves the boulevards and emerges from the rue Laffitte, all at once something opens over Paris and Notre-Dame-de-Lorette is bathed in sun.

It is half-past twelve; this seems like a good time. She won't go to the post office: long-distance calls take so long to connect that she prefers to wait in the ambience of a café rather than in a public place.

Receiver at her ear, she hears the distant voice of an old woman asking whom she is calling. As she speaks his name for the first time Marie hears her own voice sounding quite different from usual.

In a few moments, no doubt, she will have to say it again, to its owner, to confirm the identity of the person she'll be speaking to; and she will also have to give her own name. At this thought, an inexplicable fear rises within her. But now the receiver is emitting another sound, a slight intake of breath followed by a single word that fills it with an entire presence: 'Hello?'

'Hello ...'

The other voice enquires, confidently: 'How are you?'

'I'm fine ... I was calling you because ...'

Marie is about to babble on nervously, but the voice interrupts, saving her yet again.

'I can come to Paris, though it's not desperately convenient – that is unless you'd like to come here – we could have twenty-four hours together, in this town that you've never visited before ...'

She wasn't expecting him to suggest this alternative, and stammered out a vague reply that betrayed her fear of embarking on such an impetuous journey.

He said: 'OK, I'll take the first train to Paris. Come and meet me at the station.'

'I'll be there.'

The line goes dead. Thinking of the decision that he has just taken, at such speed, and comparing it with her own indecisiveness, Marie feels ashamed.

She goes back into the main room of the café and

asks for a train timetable. A train will leave in barely three-quarters of an hour ...

Outside the church is still shining bright. To her right the rue du Faubourg Montmartre, the rue Pelletier and the rue de Maubeuge are also bathed in sun. She feels as though the carrefour de Chateaudun is spreading out like the branches of a star, gently reawakening to life.

CHAPTER ELEVEN

THIS STATION seemed more attractive than the other one: more spacious, brighter, better designed. Its entrance halls didn't open directly on to the street: a big deserted forecourt isolated it from the city, creating an island of arrival and departure and emphasising the gravity of a station's status.

Marie was waiting on the platform; it was cold, and she turned up the collar of her winter coat. It suddenly struck her, with some amazement, that the person she should be looking for in the crowd was not the tanned young man in a light jacket that she had known on holiday. But when he stepped off the train and walked towards her, she didn't notice whether he was wearing a coat nor whether his skin was paler than before. She saw him, he was there, and that was all that mattered.

They shook hands without a word. Crossing the fore-court, they left the station side by side, and walked along the streets in silence.

Then Marie said: 'Perhaps you're hungry, after your journey?'

He said yes, he was. It was lunch time, so it was all perfectly logical; yet it seemed strange to her that he was hungry and that she had dared ask him about it. She let him order the meal, listening to the way he talked to other people. She noticed that he preferred hors-d'oeuvres to soup, and for the first time she watched him eat. She looked at his town clothes, at the buttoned-up collar of his blue cotton shirt, at the dark, red-striped tie. There was the uncertain, unreal world of the holiday, which she had known, and there was the everyday, real life about which she knew nothing what-soever. A daily life, full of signs, that he has only recently left in order to come to her.

On the lapel of his jacket there gleams a university badge. She can't see it clearly; she would have to lean forward, reach out her hand and pull the tiny object towards her. She does not dare touch this first secret. She lets herself wander down familiar paths: she looks at the fine, firm, rather bony face, at the delicate muscles stretched by the broad, always solemn, smile. She lingers for ages on his long, pointed chin, which stands out so well from his neck, and on his thin, sinuous mouth. She knows all about the suppleness of his thick hair; she knows, too, that his eyes never lose their profound lucidity. And yet, something new has permeated his features.

It seems to her that he is even thinner than before, or perhaps he is simply worn out, either from his first days of study or from this sudden journey. Fatigue touches his young face, without causing any damage.

They speak very little, and then only of things that do not matter. There are no tender gestures, no tender words. They keep the mystery of their lives tight, like a second presence – because a little time has passed, and because their first coming together has been incorporated into their lives, leaving a mark of which the other can have no knowledge. Do they even know themselves? If they spoke to each other more seriously, they would only be able to ask questions. And they share a passion for silence.

Here they are again in the street, side by side, treading the same furrow of life – without tenderness, without cries, without conspiratorial looks, anxiety, or remorse. In spite of the great unknown ahead of them, in spite of the torpor that has suddenly invaded their thoughts, they feel calm and strong. They know that whatever dangers might rise up to confront them, they would be courageous and powerful.

Do they also know that this same strength that sometimes permeates everything is also a sign of fate? And if they do not know this, do they know that we all carry fate inside us, like a grace, and that it is our responsibility to fulfil it?

SIDE BY SIDE, keeping in step, they walk along the streets until the place de l'Opéra sparkles in front of them. Here, without really knowing why, they come to a stop, in a brightly coloured place serving fruit juice that suddenly appeals to them. Once again they find themselves sitting opposite each other, in the same strange torpor.

Looking at Marie he smiles and says: 'How are you?'

Her voice heavy, she replies: 'I'm all right ...'

A little later, as if attempting to explain the ineffable, she says: 'It's like adjusting to a new landscape ...'

He answers in the same simple tones that she has used: 'A landscape where memories must die.'

Words that initiated and clarified nothing. All around them things are changing shape – the anticipation, the suspense of this strange land, so full of silent things. Where would it lead them – to future offers? to richness? to setbacks? to joy, surely? This new land contained an unknown power which held them both in its sway. It also held all the sweetness of a promise.

THE RUE LAFAYETTE IS LONG, and they walk its entire length, at speed. After a while they begin to pant, and because they are not speaking they can hear the sound of each other's breath. The church which shone so brightly this morning is now merely a dark shape; they pass along one side of it, then turn into a street that they follow together for the second time.

The door that opened on to a brightly lit corridor one night in September is today closed.

They do not slacken their pace, and nothing in their movements betrays the astonishment they feel when confronted by this little mystery. It could have been awkward – but Marie notices only that he now turns his head from time to time: she feels that he is looking for something. They have passed the door and are, quite simply, continuing their fast walk. When, a few moments later, he'll place his hand on her shoulder, its soft pressure will tell her he has made his choice and they can again call a halt.

THEY SAT ON A VERY LOW BED, at some distance from each other, but their hands were joined. They stayed like that, overwhelmed by this thing inside them, this thing they could not give a name to. They were overwhelmed by themselves.

Marie turned her head towards him, took this new face in her hands. 'Have you changed?' she asked, in an anguished voice. 'I can't seem to find you again …'

'No, I haven't changed,' he replied. 'Perhaps I've developed.'

It was the reply of a very young man. She couldn't stop herself smiling, but she felt a profound tenderness arising in her. She pulled his big smooth face closer to her, and kissed him, quite chastely, on the forehead.

They suddenly embraced violently, and immediately recaptured all their passion. But the sea which carried them off this evening was different from the profound depths of joy they had felt on the first night. Tonight, tumultuous waves envelop them, making them pitch, throwing them on to their sides, their backs. They utter no cries or moans, but their silent lips render ever more poignant the prolonged moan of their struggling bodies. They sink in water pockets;

groundswells bring them brusquely to the surface only to roll them back again, throwing their heads to the right and then to the left. Hands clutching shoulders, ankles joined, limbs that would never ever disentangle; they want to die together or to let the sea abandon them, rescued, on the same shore.

When, finally, the storm subsides, they still don't know where they are. They know only that they have opened their eyes together, and that they have landed. But their legs and arms do not leave each other straight away – they remain entangled, as though still enveloped by damp seaweed.

He has a secret little nickname for Marie: it's only an adjective, perhaps one that all men use; but he pronounces it in a special way, stressing the consonant as if it were two syllables. She repeats the name in reply – it's the same one she uses for him.

'What is happening to us?' she says.

'I don't know ...'

He lifts the sheets up towards her, gently, as far as her shoulders, but keeping her close to him. They sleep. How heavily they sleep that second night! Marie no longer has the look of a wild young warrior; this time, no lightning has burned their eyes. As they sleep, their features show signs of fatigue, their faces are more sorrowful, more human. How deep their second night is!

THEY GOT UP LATE – it was already lunch time, and their young stomachs were starving. They ate ravenously and single-mindedly. In the afternoon they talked a little more, but not about anything that related to themselves.

The same torpor soon enveloped them again, and each began to fear that the other was bored. At that point they felt a doleful desire to run away, to be free of each other, but the next moment they were back together again, sitting in front of hot drinks that went cold as they stared at each other with a hard expression in their eyes.

It was getting late and the departure of the last train was, cruelly, about to release them. Once again they crossed the big deserted forecourt. They had arrived a little early; they walked backwards and forwards in small steps along the platform. They discussed no dates, took no steps at all to ensure that they might meet again.

The train was ready to leave. Standing on the step his gaze took in Marie's whole body; she looked into his eyes, but held them only for a moment: the train was leaving. He closed the door, did not lean out of the window. Marie stood absolutely still and followed the long, faceless train with her eyes until the very last moment.

CHAPTER TWELVE

J EAN CAME BACK from Maubeuge with the dreaded news: the following month he and Marie would have to move there for an as yet indefinite length of time.

A host of friends descended on the household wanting to make the most of Jean and Marie's final weeks in Paris; they took up all their evenings. These were noisy times, and Marie became bored with having to listen to so-called intellectual discussions whilst records blared out incessantly, and glasses were filled and refilled. Around midnight or one o'clock, someone would say that the evening could not end so soon. Jean, uplifted by this orgy of pleasure, would propose new places they could go on to: looking exhausted, their enjoyment over, they'd trawl through the city. With luck, they might manage a new wave of excitement if one of the party, laughing uproariously, gesticulated at the long line of Hachette press lorries as they drove at full speed along the rue du Louvre. The night would always climax in a cacophony of delight when they reached Les Halles and saw the beautiful vegetables piled up in the icy dawn. These wan-looking creatures, who knew each other too well, would slacken their pace and look behind them, awaiting Marie. Then, overcome by fatigue, they'd be invaded by a sense of sadness and regret for their wasted lives.

MARIUS DENIS WOULD TAKE Marie's arm. 'If you come back to Paris on your own from time to time, will you save your evenings for me?'

Claudine, shivering in her evening dress, would lean her head on Marie's shoulder and say: 'I know you won't write to me often. But if you managed to arrange your lessons in a bunch, say once a month, you could stay with us. You won't abandon me completely, will you, Marie? Answer me, please!'

Walking against Marie, Claudine's slight, trembling body had to endure the slow, ample pace of her sister, so ill matched to her own.

They would shake hands; some would hail taxis, while the rest stood around on the pavement in groups, waiting for more taxis to arrive.

'Marie, you'll be leaving us soon,' said a tall young man who held on to her hand a little too long. She looked at him as he went on: 'Do let us know whenever you come back!'

And Marie would feel other hands clasping her hands, and Denis's arm through hers, and the weight of Claudine's dear head on her shoulder. Already, this present seemed to be monopolising the future. She would clench her teeth to stop herself from expressing her genuine desire to be left alone. 'Please, please, leave me ...'

After a while Marie was saying no to almost all invitations and Jean went to these evenings with friends on his own. Occasionally she would go out, too, walking haphazardly through a Paris which at that time seemed to belong to her alone. She always returned home well before Jean: she would read or, almost without thinking, make various preparations for their departure, tidying drawers, making a start at packing the cases.

TIME PASSED SLOWLY; Jean was late. Marie suffered at the thought that he was enjoying himself without her, abandoning herself to a mood that still betrayed signs of the self-absorbed nature of her love. She waited for him without doing anything else. When he finally returned she'd take his beloved, familiar face in her hands and say: 'How you wear yourself out!'

'Are you cross?'

'No, of course not.'

On his way to the bedroom, Jean would call: 'Are you coming to bed, too, Marie?'

'No, not yet.'

And she'd stay there until the blue light of dawn came through the window. Thrown back on herself, she'd feel quite alone at the heart of a well-worn past – even though she had created such fine things. Jean, Claudine: links that did not want to expire, that tightened their hold in a final struggle as others tried to replace them.

'Please, please leave me!' She'd have liked to shout this in all the space around her. How she longed to have neither past nor future! And yet – on the one hand there were these still burning ashes and on the other there was this new thing, this thing that did not yet have a name. Like a warm beast that moved inside her, making its nest.

ONE EVENING IN THE STUDY, sorting out some papers she wanted to take with her, she came across an old letter from herself to Claudine. She remembered having written it during a short holiday she'd spent away from her family with some friends of her father's.

Describing her journey to the provinces she wrote: 'I have a sudden desire for solitude. I take precautions to be alone in my compartment: I shut the door to the corridor, I pull the curtains. People try to open it, they go on trying, then I hear them say: "Let's give up." Oh, the joy of being alone in this train that is three-quarters full! Now, for me, life is somewhere else, at the end of this railway journey …'

She told Claudine about the days passed so far away, about her delight in discovering a town that was unknown to her: 'It is a town that is beautiful in its huge size, beautiful for its stillness, its quiet streets, its big regular houses, its well-placed lights; in the colour of the night all is absence, absence of expectation even. A fixed calm arises from this town that I have ended up loving dearly, loving too much even, for its still, dangerous beauty.'

Such a young letter – and yet Marie liked it because it brought back her whole adolescence: her need for solitude, for an intense life, and that special fear of loving too much. She liked its youthful, graceful awkwardness of expression. And its description of a provincial town conjured up the image of another ... All these things superimposed themselves on one another in her heart, as if they were related.

She re-read those short verbless sentences, so common among the two sisters when they wrote to each other; curtailed propositions, as if thrown in by chance, but which were always subtle allusions to everything that Marie and Claudine had said, and which carried a heavy weight of meaning: 'The splendour of life: failure is not permitted. Life is reality, it does not allow for the imagination. I think of a book I love which ends with the phrase, "Beware of the flight of steps."'

This book was one that she and Claudine had often discussed, and the sentence had haunted Marie's adolescence. What had she meant to convey to Claudine when she quoted it that day? The letter was not finished ...

She anxiously scrutinised the hasty writing that had produced the last sentence; it wasn't yet the writing of a woman. These days she understood all too well the deep wound you can inflict on yourself if you fall on the last step; but she also knew that she had now rejected the world of myth. Whatever remained from the past would have to be respected as reality. And facing her lay the delicious dangers of fatality, into which she had to advance with an open heart. You had to become, not simply to be.

Marie stayed like this, reflecting, for a long time. She was still holding in her hands the pages she had just read, as she leaned her beautiful thirty-year-old face on a letter by a seventeen year old. There was a fine, deep serenity inside her that night, as an image from the past was superseded and given new meaning by the reality of the present.

It seemed to Marie, immobile at the top of the steps, that she was holding the lamp up high for herself so that she could safely make her descent.

CHAPTER THIRTEEN

'Shall we take the little desk?'
'The less furniture the better, you know that. But then ...'

'It's so pretty!'

'OK, let's take it. The tenants might damage it.'

Jean and Marie hadn't given up their apartment. The current state of Jean's finances had meant that they were forced to take the most economical option: at Maubeuge, they would occupy a floor of his parents' house, and since this meant they wouldn't need much furniture, they would sublet the Paris apartment.

Marie opened the drawers of the desk and emptied them, then took hold of the desk by the edge of a shelf and carried it, with her strong arms, into another room, depositing it among baskets full of clothes and kitchen equipment.

Drawing breath, she looked around her at the filled cases, ready to be taken away.

Leaving Paris to go and live in Maubeuge, like a prisoner. She saw dark days to come, days that would stifle her ... She left the room and came back with a pile of books. She placed them in a trunk which was only half full, covering them with a towel, and then stopped again. She must make plans to escape from Maubeuge. Yes, the idea would be to bunch the lessons: two hours at a time for each student every two weeks; parents would accept that. Thursdays would be best: she could have one pupil in the morning and two in the afternoon, even three; she must pack in as many as possible.

She could leave Maubeuge by the first train in the morning and return in the evening. Even allowing for the travel costs, there would be quite a bit left over; everyone would agree. And she could write articles for the magazine: at last Denis would serve some sort of function, why not? And as for the money she would earn, she'd ask Jean if she could keep some small part of it for herself. This way, every month, or every other month, she could stay in Paris a little longer than the time strictly necessary for the lessons, and no one would have any claims on her. For one day, or maybe two, she would be alone, with no witness other than herself.

And then – but that was already the future; she ought to stop there, without imagining anything. The future would look after itself, day by day. She would struggle, she knew that: tomorrow might be fine, but for now, there was today to cope with. The present meant finishing this move and following Jean to Maubeuge and being by his side, because she loved him with such a profound tenderness. Tomorrow would be fine but the present mattered, too. Packing the trunks, leaving Paris, spending dark days in Maubeuge … Courage! Move on!

Marie was on her knees in front of the wicker trunk; after checking one more time that the books had been properly wedged in, she lifted the lid and secured it with an iron bar. She stood up, resting her hands on the trunk, in a brisk movement that made the wicker creak.

She found Jean sorting the papers in the desk. Observing that she was looking around her to see whether any important object was being overlooked, he pointed towards a corner of the room. 'Are we taking that?'

'Certainly we are! We'll need it!'

Laughing, she picked up the big chess set with its shiny wooden figures and held them in front of her. Jean stopped her halfway and made a face: 'We're going to be bored to death, aren't we?'

Marie leaned over to him and gave him a big, broad kiss on the cheek. 'Of course not – you and I can never be bored.'

THEY TOOK AN EVENING TRAIN, a fast one: Paris was ever further away. You could hardly see anything through the windows: from time to time, a few lights would delineate the invisible landscape. The distance increased instead of diminishing; Marie could feel the kilometres mounting up. Everything that was behind her seemed so small.

She looked at the man sitting opposite her. She looked at his strong jaw, his mop of hair. His head was in a newspaper; he was reading with one eyebrow raised, and there were lines on his forehead. He was her husband; and she expected neither joy nor sorrow from her love for him. But she loved him with a friendship in which the flesh was implicated, too: she desired for his happiness in a spiritual as well as a physical sense. He was her dearly beloved brother. He was a friend whose face, arms, legs, veins, blood, and everything that made him live, were so precious to her that they constituted a potential source of sorrow. Her husband: the phrase might also have meant intoxication, desire, love; and that would have been infinitely beautiful. Or again, it might have implied indifference, which would have been easier: this was neither one thing nor the other. It was just something else, for better or for worse – this was how it was. And the number of kilometres continued to increase …

'You're not cold, Jean?'

He raised his head: 'No, I'm fine. What about you, darling?'

'I'm fine, too.'

He buried himself in the paper again.

No, she wasn't cold. Her forehead burned and neither her hands nor her shoulders nor her legs were cold. But her heart, the whole of her heart, was frozen stiff. It felt like a hard, painful block of ice.

She leaned her head on the wall of the compartment and closed her eyes. Put your hands on my heart, my beloved.

Don't say that, you mustn't say that. Everything is so far away. Iron curtain, silence, farewells without a future. But what about that warm beast stirring inside her, who claims her name? Don't say that. It cannot move. The train carries on, while people and places disappear somewhere over there. What does it matter? 'Life is elsewhere, at the end of the journey.' Let the beast lie low, induced into a state of lethargy, surrounded by cold. Calm, empty, heart of ice. But wait, that is not my heart! That heart isn't mine! Don't speak. Everything is so far away. And the distance is diminishing; Maubeuge is getting nearer. So be it. But where, then, is all the world's tenderness?

A fine rain streaked noiselessly against the windows of the compartment. Jean raised his head and said: 'It's started. When I'm going away from Paris, it always begins to rain at this point in the journey – I told you!'

Marie looked out: the wet windows hid only a night without light. She closed her eyes again.

It is raining on Saint-Quentin, on Maubeuge, on Feignies. A sad, soft rain, somewhat harsher, that extends over the whole of Belgium as far as the end of the Ardennes, where the earth is rough and red and where the rainclouds are so low that they brush against the branches of black spruce trees, like fog. If only the train would go right past Maubeuge, and carry straight on ... Do hearts find peace in the wet, sad north, with its faded colours, its vast, desolate, marshy solitude?

Perhaps it is raining still, further away, on the wide river where deserted cliffs carry the Wagnerian names of dead goddesses. Perhaps, in the presence of such heart-rending mournfulness, my heart might resign itself to death.

'WAKE UP, MARIE, we're at Maubeuge! You've slept practically the whole time. You really overtired yourself, what with all the packing and the suitcases.'

'It was nothing, Jean, really.'

'But it is. While we're here you're going to rest properly, I mean it.'

Marie takes the luggage down from the rack and buttons up her coat. Jean wipes the window, leans his forehead against it and, cupping his hands, looks out for landmarks: 'Still a few minutes to go.'

She sits down again and lets her hands fall open on to her knees; she's tired, and her head is empty. She's waiting.

ON THE PLATFORM Jean looked around the throng of people and said excitedly: 'There's Papa!'

Marie kissed his father, let him take a suitcase, let him take an arm. As they pass in front of the station café, she thinks how she would love to go in, order a coffee, smoke a cigarette. If anyone knew what she was thinking, it would seem ridiculous.

'It's not far,' Jean's father said. 'We can walk.'

She lagged a little behind them. He went on: 'Come on now, children! You're expected at home.' And he pushed her forward. Jean and his father were talking, giving each other news about the running of the factory. It was late and they were walking through a town which was completely deserted at night. At the corner of a street she saw a little café with a brightly lit front; again she felt a strange temptation to go in, to have a cigarette and a cup of coffee. At other tables, unknown men would be talking – fragments of sentences that she would pick up and reconstruct, so that she could guess at their lives.

The factory loomed up out of the night. Their three silhouettes, dark and silent, moved past the railings, then round a tall heap of scrap iron or coke – it was hard to tell which in the dark. They walked by the side of a long, windowless wall, then came to the house, overshadowed by the ungainly outline of the factory.

Jean's mother, a small, round woman, was already in the corridor to greet them. She rushed here and there, kissing them several times, making no secret of her pleasure at seeing them. When she had ushered them in and taken their coats, she looked at Marie and said: 'I always want to say how much you've grown!'

Marie let herself be looked at, let herself be kissed. There was a strange, musty smell in that house; she wondered whether it came from the house itself or whether it was the greasy smell of the machines that penetrated as far as this. The little woman was talking to her again: 'And then there's your meals – we can sort that out easily – there's no point in you working separately in your apartment – we can make a big soup, for everybody, down here. Do you prefer to have it in the evening, or at midday?'

Marie turned away with a wild smile, letting the question hang in the air. From morning till night, she thought, these hands were going to want to help her, these eyes were going to follow her movements, this mouth was going to speak to her; this heart was going to demand that they did the housework together. She loathed this woman, a sudden witness to her everyday life.

Jean looked at her, saw her face tense up and thought to himself: God, she's difficult.

But seeing the look on Jean's face and the astonishment of the little grey woman who stood there, expecting her to be delighted by what she had just said, Marie turned back and managed to summon up a sweeter smile: 'How kind you are, Mama, you've made us a hot meal – and at this hour!'

BEFORE EATING Jean and Marie went upstairs to leave their suitcases on the first floor, in the rooms that they were to occupy. Their bedroom was scarcely appealing: old and grim. Marie looked round, wondering what she could do to alter it. Jean was sitting at the edge of the bed – dismayed by the ambience, suddenly fed up with the whole situation, he was reduced to silence.

Marie went up to him and said: 'Come on, don't be depressed. It's only a period in our lives, one that will pass. It'll just be for a few months. We'll get by. And if it goes on, we can rent an apartment, if you don't like it here. Besides, I can transform this place. You'll see, in a few days it'll be much nicer.'

Looking at her, Jean already felt less unhappy. She took him by the wrists and forced him down on to the bed. 'Now, young man, I am going to make you laugh. I'm going to give you some Swedish gymnastics ...'

She pulled his arms, upwards, downwards, from both sides, then brought them back to his chest. Releasing him, she slipped her hand under his shirt, along the sides of his body. She tickled him, then took his hands and started the exercise again: 'One, two ... one, two ...'

They ran out of breath and Jean laughed like a child. She climbed on the bed next to him, showering him with a whole raft of quick little kisses – on his chin, his cheeks, his forehead. She ruffled his hair with both hands, laughing to see him in this state. She let her head fall back on his broad shoulders. Her left hand stayed in his hair; against her right hand, she felt his heart beat regularly. Suddenly she straightened up, raised her voice: 'And what about your mama's hot dinner?'

They got up and, seeing Jean's untidy hair in the mirror, laughed again.

'Comb your hair quickly,' she said, 'and go down. I'll follow you soon.'

When he'd shut the door behind him, she sat down on the bed, covered her face with her hands and wept. In a tearful, halting voice, she whispered to herself, behind her hands: 'It's not right to cry like this; not right.' Fearing that Jean would come back up to find her, she groped her way to the door and turned the key. She stood there with her face buried in her arms, which were crossed against the door.

Now that she was alone, she had no option but to give in to the pressure of her grief.

Still panting, she made her way to the washbasin, did her hair, powdered her nose, composed her face. Opening the door she gave out a deep sigh, as though to liberate herself tearlessly from a final sob.

On the floor below, they were waiting for her before serving the late meal. When she sat down to eat, Jean felt he could draw reassurance from the calm, almost joyful expression on her face.

THE NEXT DAY a van turned up, bringing the writing desk, several cases and a few more bits of furniture. Marie helped unload and carry them into the house, her hands blue with cold. She put the furniture in place and sorted the clothes, the pots and pans, the books. She spent the day doing this, and in the days that followed she continued to sort, sweep, hammer nails and attach pictures to walls. Jean was quite satisfied with the apartment now, seeing it inhabited by objects that he knew well. Not so Marie: the place may have been transformed, but deep inside her nothing had changed at all.

ONE MORNING at about six o'clock Jean and Marie were awoken by the telephone: a long, vibrant, urgent ringing.

'Must be long-distance,' Jean said, getting out of bed.

The phrase shocked Marie rigid. She got up, wanting to run to the phone, but Jean stopped her: 'Don't worry, I'll go.

If it's for Papa, I'll shout up, and you can go and get him.'

She had no reason to feel so disturbed; she knew that it was impossible for it to be anything to do with *that*. But the feeling was stronger than she, and her heart beat violently. She waited impatiently. When the ringing stopped, she could hear Jean's voice, calm and neutral, saying: 'Yes, I can hear you ... Yes, it's me. What's the matter?' A pause, then, incredulously: 'Are you sure she's not just asleep?' More concerned now, and in a muffled voice: 'Yes, yes, all right, there's no doubt about it ... yes. What's she taken? You don't know ... Food poisoning? Seems pretty unlikely to me, old chap.' The voice making an effort to sound stronger now: 'Let's hope she'll be all right ... Yes, of course ... Phone us again if there is the slightest change in her condition. Don't tell her mother yet. No, nor her father, let Marie decide about that.'

At his final words Marie grasped the situation in a flash. Claudine! She dashed down the staircase, snatched the receiver from Jean's hands and cried out, in anger and in pain: 'What has she taken? For heaven's sake look in her room!'

But Claudine's husband had hung up, and all she heard was a slight crackling on the line. Jean said: 'He doesn't know what she's taken, but he's called the doctor – he'll know. When Armand came home yesterday evening he thought she was asleep. He went to bed and didn't realise until this morning that her sleeping wasn't normal. He wasted time trying to wake her up ... called the doctor first, and then us, straight away.'

Marie interrupted: 'When's the next train to Paris?'

'At half-past, but you won't catch it, my poor love, you should wait for the …'

'I will catch it.'

Marie rushed up the stairs, pulled her overcoat over her nightdress, put on her shoes. Picking up a small suitcase that was still in the bedroom, she threw in some underwear and a dress, and checked in her bag that she had enough money for the journey.

'I'll call you from Paris,' she said.

And she ran all the way to the station.

CHAPTER FOURTEEN

S HE TOOK HER SEAT without noticing where it was situated, which carriage it was in. Little by little, she recovered her breath.

Everything was bathed in light – meadows, factories, stations, villages – but she didn't look out. What was the point of all this rush, she wondered: this haste, this dash to the station? Whatever had happened to Claudine, it was too late to do anything about it now. 'You won't abandon me completely, will you, Marie? Answer me, please!' In a sudden movement she pressed her head against the train window, letting her eyes wander but not seeing anything: she didn't even register the way her forehead bumped against the glass.

She hadn't brought any cigarettes, and a need for the taste of smoke engulfed her to the point of pain. She needed to feel that slight burning in the throat as the puffs slid down;

more seriously, she needed a dose of nicotine in her blood.

It occurred to her that since she had brought some underwear and a dress, she could go and quickly get dressed in the lavatory; it would also be a relief to clean her teeth. But she didn't move, she just pulled the folds of her coat more tightly over her knees. What had Claudine taken? Armand hadn't a clue, but they must surely know by now.

Did it really matter whether she had taken this or that? Yes, it did. This is the way women always do it – poison, gas, or drowning: few have the courage to use a revolver. In the end, few women have the courage to live …

Marie felt a silent anger rising up from the very depths of her outrage. Suicide in the face of problems, or suicide in the face of great distress … Refusing to struggle, refusing to be alone, refusing to suffer: it's all refusal, all along the way! When women suffer, when they are hurt, what do they do? Cut their losses, that's what. A cowardly flight towards peace, towards annihilation … Is there nothing to stop them, no quality independent of all others, that makes each person a unique individual, that should always prevent people from killing themselves? A very precious quality that should be carried forward, like a priest waving incense?

Marie turned back towards the window. The landscape was rushing past, moving quickly away from the gaze of this woman with her broad, hard forehead, her wide-open, fiery eyes. Intense thoughts, precise as commands, filled with determination as well as with anger, hammered at her mind and at her heart. 'You must commit. Right up to the last minute you must struggle against the enemy, against death; you must struggle until it takes you by force and you have to surrender! The crime is to give in. You must not desert; you must be on the side of life.'

THIS WAS THE POINT that Claudine, in her desperation and hopelessness, had reached. Marie thought of the wretched little face she loved so much, of her hesitant walk; she thought of that fine sunny morning when Claudine had complained of feeling cold and Marie had lit a fire. Marie was no longer reflecting; just as she had dashed down the stairs in her desperate need to catch that train, to be by her side, she now had only one thought, only one desire. She closed her eyes, burning with tears. Why doesn't the train go faster, faster, faster? She wants to feel that hot little body beneath her fingers; she wants to see those child's breasts rise up again …

A door opened, and someone walked across the wide vehicle; like all trains on the northern network, it had no corridor. There was a slight stirring, and one or two people got to their feet. The train was coming to a halt. Even those who were not getting off moved around, standing in front of windows and opening them, looking at the station. Marie could hold out no longer. She leaned towards a fellow traveller and, with excessive politeness, asked him for a cigarette. He gave her one and lit it. 'It's no fun travelling alone,' he said. 'Much nicer to be able to talk to someone.' Seeing that Marie had retreated into herself, smoking nervously, he dared say no more.

The train set off again.

CHAPTER FIFTEEN

Armand and the doctor turn round as Marie enters the bedroom but she moves straight to the foot of the bed without a word. She was expecting to see a ghostly pallor, but only Claudine's forehead is pale: her cheeks are dark red, almost violet. She is lying on her back, half-naked. She does not move, but Marie can tell that she is alive.

'We've been working on her for two hours,' Armand says desperately.

'She's in a comatose sleep,' says the doctor in a matter-of-fact voice.

Marie sees the basin full of water, the wet towel, the broken ampoules, the syringe leaning against its box, needle in the air. She takes these things in quickly, then looks at Claudine, and finally back at the doctor: she wants to gaze at him, to read his face. But he's paying no attention to the people standing up; he's leaning over the sleeping body, opening Claudine's eyelids with his thumb and index finger. Now Marie understands why her cheeks are so red: he is slapping her, with stronger and stronger blows, first one side and then the other – her little head shakes back and forth between his big male hands. Marie watches, her teeth clenched, her hands clutching the wooden bed.

At last he stops, opening the eyelids and feeling the pulse. Marie still says nothing, thinks nothing, though every move he makes strikes deep into her heart. He mutters, as if to himself: 'But she moved, a while ago …'

The doctor takes Claudine's wrist between his fingers again and holds it there for a long time. He stands up and lets an odd humming sound emerge from his lips, as if wanting to distract himself; then, moving fast, he picks up his prescription book and writes some words in it. He looks at Marie, assesses her, hands her the sheet. 'How far is the pharmacy?'

'About ten minutes.'

He gestures towards her with his hand; he's uncertain, thinks aloud: 'Getting there, coming back, warming it up …' He shrugs. 'No. Bring me some warm water, kitchen salt, and an injecting tube.'

Marie goes into the bathroom then runs towards the kitchen.

Armand gets up from his chair and moves towards the bed. 'Are things not going well?'

'Yes, they're fine!' In other words: 'Go back to your chair and get off my back.'

Armand had never understood much of Claudine's character. Nine years ago, her youth came charging into his forty years: bedazzled by her nervous, dreamy, disconcerting nature, he'd indulged her every whim. When he saw her unhappy or suffering, he'd sit down with hands on knees and eyes full of fear, like a lost old man. A decent sort, Armand. Decent, but sad.

Scarcely five minutes later Marie came back into the bedroom with the things the doctor had asked for.

'Put them on the table,' he said. Looking at the injecting tube he asked: 'Was it clean?'

'Yes, I poured boiling water on it before filling it up with warm.'

Marie's voice is calm, and her movements have a perfect precision. Her face is set, and her uncombed hair, with its curls lying crushed and flat around her brow, make her look harder than ever, cruel almost. She may be impassive; she is also pathetically pale.

The doctor prepared the solution. He said: 'Squeeze the tube,' as he removed the ebonite valve.

It took only a few seconds to fix a whole array of tubes and a needle. Now Claudine is exposed: her nightdress is rolled up to her groin, revealing her skinny legs and her kneecaps, which make two little angular protrusions. Her skin is still light brown, but changes colour slightly in the middle of her thighs, a souvenir of the shorts she wore in the holiday sun three months ago.

'Let go of the tube,' said the doctor, 'and lift up the nozzle.'

Marie obeyed.

'I should have asked you to bring a nail and a hammer …'

'We'll manage,' she replied. 'I'd waste too much time looking for them.'

They have both forgotten the presence of Armand.

'Lift it higher … yes, that's fine.'

The water flows through incredibly slowly; there is no noise in the bedroom, and Marie's arm is going numb. The skin on Claudine's thigh rises and swells, and around the needle, which is fixed like a little steel arrow, a lump develops and expands. Marie can hear the movement of her heart inside her own body; while the doctor feels Claudine's pulse, she mechanically counts her own heartbeats.

Raising her left arm she carefully passes the receptacle from one hand to the other. Now that her right arm is free, she stretches it out along her body, shakes it a little, lifts it up again and places her hand beneath the bottom of the receptacle. Once more she looks at the broken ampoules on the table: there are four or five of them, flung back carelessly into a metal container. Because of their position it's not possible to read their labels at a glance; from the little heap she can make out one letter here and another there. She pieces together the word 'arsenic'. A deadly dose intended to save Claudine, to combat what she has taken. But what has she taken? And now these two litres of salt water. All that inside Claudine's body.

Claudine wanted to kill herself; Claudine has deserted life. What has she taken? Why has she taken it? Did she want to die because she knew that she was spoiling the life that had been given her, thinking she was unworthy of the gift? Marie's mind has gone to work again, and this idea has seized her so strongly, like vertigo, that she staggers around in it for several seconds. She sees Claudine stretched out, cheeks very pale; Claudine dead, as if surrounded by a halo. 'Look at me, Marie, and admire me, at last.' There she is, undressed, smacked on the cheek, knocked about, her body filled with two counter poisons, her blood heavy with salt water. They are denying her gesture, dragging her against her will, bringing her back by force, feeble and unworthy, to the bosom of what she had tried to respect.

'Marie, my friend, my sister, stick up for me … Let me keep the only real gesture I have ever made in my whole life.' Marie's heart beats faster; for the first time since she has come into the bedroom her face loses its impassivity. The doctor raises his eyes to hers: 'How much more is there?'

Marie lowers the injecting tube and looks at it. 'About a litre.'

'Let's carry on, then.'

He leans towards Claudine again, to check her eyes and her pulse, to apply a little massage to the swelling in her thigh. He is alert to the tiniest signs given out by this body, to what is left of its life: he wants to open up this remainder, to preserve and increase it. In one leap Marie's heart takes its place again, next to this man, in the attempt to save her sister's body.

There is still life there, do you hear me? I don't want to see you dead, even if your face is at peace. I don't want to admire you in death, because there is nothing great in death when whatever preceded it was even less. I don't want to defend you, I can't save you in death. You must see, Claudine, my sister, my friend – I'm on the side of life …

'The level of the water is going down: lift it a bit higher,' the doctor said.

Marie raises both hands again, above her head: they are so cold and stiff that they can no longer feel the weight of the receptacle. From her uplifted arms all feeling has gone; pain has become a fixture. Her heart is now beating quite regularly and her face, so pale today, has resumed its fixed, implacable look.

The water flows with infinite slowness, and it will perhaps take as long for Claudine's life to return. Perhaps her life will return as gently as this.

NIGHT FALLS EARLY at this time of year; even though it was only three o'clock, it was already getting dark. Marie drew the curtains and lit the lamps. 'There's nothing more I can do for the moment,' the doctor said. 'Little by little she'll begin to wake up. This evening I'll come back.'

He had picked up his instruments from the table and was packing his bag. Marie asked: 'How did you find out what she had taken?'

Fumbling in his pocket he pulled out two glass phials and threw them on to the table. 'I found these at the back of the fireplace. They always hide them there, in the ashes.'

As he left the room he added: 'Above all don't leave her. If she goes completely still, you know what to do.'

Marie went back into the bedroom to find Armand with one hand on Claudine's inert arm; with the other hand he was holding the two glass phials left behind by the doctor and looking at them uncertainly. 'Do you have any idea, Marie, why she would do a thing like that?'

'Do a thing like that?' Marie repeated his words with a sad smile. 'That' encompassed so many things, including Armand himself.

He was completely exhausted with worry and incomprehension. Marie spoke to him briefly, to reassure him, then sent him to lie down in a nearby room.

She sat on the edge of the bed to watch over her sister as the doctor had recommended. At times Claudine's head would move gently, a little to the right and then a little to the left, or she would attempt to move and let her hand fall, or her whole body would be seized by trembling. The first time she went totally still, for several long moments, Marie shook her by the shoulders, repeating, 'Claudine! Claudine!' Then, since she still wasn't moving, she reached towards the hot, red cheeks and slapped them, gently. As if explaining her actions, she said to her several times: 'You mustn't sleep; you mustn't …' Then she hit her harder and harder, bravely, for several minutes.

It was time, now, that flowed with such infinite slowness. Outside, it had long been dark, and Marie was still at her post. Claudine's arms were stretching out ever further and the trembling of her body was turning into real movements. From time to time she would let out a light groan, a little guttural complaint; from time to time her chest rose and, in an agony of tension, let out a hiccup, and Marie would wipe a greenish foam from her pale lips, her chin, her neck, from her childish breast, now gently calming down. Or was it calming down too much? Once again Marie would hold and strike Claudine's prostrate, exhausted body, that had already been battered both by herself and by the work of her saviours. And again Marie would say, in a mother's voice: 'Claudine, my little one, you must not sleep …'

CHAPTER SIXTEEN

THIS WENT ON all through the night.

The next day, Claudine opened her heavy eyelids every now and again and tried to look at Marie. Several times those painful spasms rose up from her stomach, still drenched in poison. When someone spoke to her, she made signs to show that she had understood, and a few slow words emerged from her swollen lips.

Marie sorted out some clean clothes for her, tidied her hair, brought a basin of warm water and washed her all over. Whether her woman's body had been disturbed by this shock to the system or whether it was simply that time of the month, Claudine had started a period: as Marie squeezed the sponge in the basin, the water was pink on her hands. She wrapped Claudine in a blanket and, while the cleaner changed the bedclothes, sat the poor little wretch on her knee. Although Claudine, at thirty-two, was older than Marie, she seemed like an over-sized little girl whose feet touched the ground. Marie held her in her arms, moving her right shoulder so as to support her head naturally. She placed her lips on Claudine's forehead, on her hairline, and kept them there, moving ever so gently.

A day later Claudine was following all Marie's movements around the bedroom with her eyes. She was speaking a few words almost normally. From time to time Marie would give her something to drink, lift up her hair, puff the pillows.

Claudine took her hand and said: 'Can you understand, I felt so alone, so unhappy ... It was like a gigantic despair, a kind of fear, and also like a very deep sense of fatigue. I felt that I was finally going to be able to have a long rest ...'

Marie said nothing; she was touched to the quick by these sad, halting words.

'At the beginning of the day, when this ... when this fear became so unbearable ... if you had been in Paris, I would have called you, I would have asked you to go out with me ... If I had seen someone, perhaps I would have felt less desperate ... perhaps this need to sleep would have diminished ... I don't know ... I don't know ...'

She moved her head, shrugging her shoulders. She spoke without any sense of tragedy or regret; it was as if she wanted to explain something she didn't fully understand herself.

'That's how it came about. You mustn't think that I preferred death to life ... I wasn't thinking of either death or life … To sleep … Yes, that was what I wanted, above all to sleep …'

Marie removed her hand and said, in a voice as feeble as her sister's: 'Shush, don't think about all that. You must put that day out of your mind …'

In an appeasing caress, she gently stroked Claudine's forehead and cheek, but had to move quickly away from the bed to hide the fact that her eyes were filling with tears. Her emotions were stirred not only by Claudine's sad little voice and by her suffering but by the painful death of a last illusion.

THAT EVENING, as Claudine slept, Marie stayed by her bedside for a long time. She followed the movements of her feeble chest, she watched her closed eyelids, still a little swollen and retaining the big bluish circles she'd acquired when she was so close to death. To save Claudine … But Claudine wasn't one of those creatures whose behaviour was determined by anything that comes from the inside; for such people salvation is always false. Over and over down the years Marie had heard her say: 'Perhaps if I had a child – or if I fell seriously in love with someone …'; and she imagined the mournful pleasure that Claudine would derive from losing herself, burying herself in another human being. The thought suddenly came to her: If only there were a God …

A strange image entered her mind: a group of sad, languid young girls in the peace and quiet of a convent. With a fervour that nothing about them seems to explain, they prostrate themselves in their black garments, touching the icy flagstones with their pallid faces, their young breasts. Their eyes shine and their hands join, stretch out, interlock. They are enveloped, transfigured by love; they are invaded and uplifted by a clarity that finally gives meaning to their lives. An immense clarity that comes from elsewhere – because God, with the infinite mercy and tenderness of a creator for the whole of his creation, is calling these lost little creatures back to him. He'd said to them, as he'd said to others before them: 'I gave you flesh, heart and spirit. Go now, leave me, and try to understand the full value of my work.'

If God exists, Marie thought suddenly, it must be out of a desperate kind of love that he offers himself like this, face to face, to those who have scorned the life they have been given. Would not the real triumph of a creator come from those who love him in his work?

CHAPTER SEVENTEEN

CLAUDINE NO LONGER needed twenty-four-hour care: her sick body would recover bit by bit, almost of its own accord, in the course of a long convalescence. Marie had spoken to their mother, because it was now possible to conceal the real cause of the illness.

For the first time in six days Marie left Claudine's apartment.

SHE STARTED BY WALKING AIMLESSLY, so elated was she to rediscover the fresh air outside and the bustle of the streets – but she walked quickly, in long strides, propelled by a physical need for action and speed. By instinct she went back towards the Right Bank, to the Paris she loved: a strange quadrilateral, enlarged and heart-shaped, delineated more or less by the stations Buttes-Chaumont, Bastille, Opéra and

Clichy. This was a Paris that people who came from else-where found less than dazzling – but for Marie, it was the true heart of the city, where the streets, the houses, the bars, the people, were the most Parisian in the whole of Paris.

She soon realised she was famished. She hadn't been worried by having to eat quick snacks on the corner of a table in Claudine's apartment with the fetid smell of illness in the air: she had a good strong digestion, and she wasn't one of those people who were easily thrown by the presence of a sick body. But now that she was free, she longed for a big healthy meal again, consumed in a place she liked. She went into a restaurant in the rue des Petits-Champs and ordered meat, vegetables, cheese and cider. The thrill she felt at the taste of the fresh, sharp drink was both deep and childlike.

When she had finished her meal she lit a cigarette and smoked quietly, sitting at the table for several more minutes, enveloped in a strange sense of well-being. She was savouring her newfound freedom – and the dawn of a happiness that was beyond doubt. She had definitely made up her mind, so she could reflect confidently and calmly on the difficulties that would have to be faced.

What would she tell the others? She would say that after what she had been through with Claudine in the past few days she felt the urge to be alone, to be free for a while. She would tell them in a voice so firm and reassuring that it would be impossible to raise any objections. What about money? She had a hundred francs left. She smiled to herself: not even enough to buy the rail ticket. She thought for a few moments, looked at the ring that she wore on the third finger of her right hand, and left the restaurant.

When she walked along the rue du Cherche-Midi, a little later to turn into the rue de Rennes, she was still wearing the same satisfied little smile.

INSIDE THE BUILDING she saw a long queue of people, mainly women. When they reached the desk they deposited men's suits, old clothes, sets of cutlery, small wirelesses. While the clerk was estimating the value of an object the women didn't say anything, as if afraid of putting him in a bad mood; their demeanour was indifferent, almost nonchalant. Their eyes were beseeching, but he wasn't looking at them; by the time he raised his head to theirs he had definitively established the amount of the loan. They always accepted, the gentleness of their voices belying their sense of resignation. When someone put an object down on the desk everyone pushed forward a bit, so as to get a better view. That was the best part of it, seeing what was contained in other people's packages. At the window where you collected the money, everyone talked to each other again as they waited.

These people had all been forced there by hunger and misery. Having granted herself the right to behave in the same way, did Marie feel no shame as she slipped among them? No, none at all. If they had come to this place to be able to buy bread, she had come out of her heart's desire, to preserve a love and a deep happiness. Such things matter, too.

When it was her turn she held out her hand and said quietly: 'My ring ...'

'You need to go to the other window,' the clerk said.

People moved aside to let Marie pass, jokingly calling out to her, whistling in admiration.

'The jewellery counter – lucky you!' a man said, laughing.

She received a hundred and fifty francs, more or less the price of the rail ticket; the hundred francs she already had on her would cover the rest of the cost of the journey. She felt strangely rich.

Stopping at the post office to send a telegram, she walked slowly back to Claudine's apartment.

The next day she called Jean, kissed Claudine, pulled the door of the apartment behind her and walked out into the coldest hours of a January morning.

CHAPTER EIGHTEEN

S HE'D BEEN ON THE TRAIN for over an hour: it was so full that she was standing up in the corridor as the soldiers passed to and fro. Wanting a change of scene she made her way to the refreshment bar, which was small and packed with soldiers. She elbowed her way through all the strong shoulders, the only woman to venture into this surge of blue. At first the men were astonished, then they offered her coffee, acid drops and rough cigarettes – which she smoked in the same way as they did. She bought them beers; they chatted.

Someone was attempting to get into the refreshment car holding a dog in his arms. Trying and failing to reach the bar, he was brandishing the animal above the men as if to save it from suffocation. He needed a drink – for his dog. Marie and the soldiers took the situation over, passing the dog from hand to hand like a balloon and laughing until they cried; the fact that its owner looked so appalled only increased their mirth. The dog, a young fox terrier, was barking and generally revelling in the situation. When a handsome African soldier in a red coat lowered his beer glass to allow the dog to take a couple of sips, its master screamed with fear while Marie and the soldiers screamed with laughter.

Exit both master and dog.

In this narrow lair the atmosphere was stifling and filled with cigarette smoke. Marie stayed on, squeezed between their shoulders, struck by all the paraphernalia of leather and metal, breathing in the smell of sweat emanating from the heavy uniforms. Yet she was happy – with the heat and the smoke, with the smell of these young men all packed in together, with the deafening sound of laughter, the singing and the off-colour jokes. She was so happy that she laughed at whatever they said. Life was so sweet she would have laughed at anything. These soldiers were her companions in joy; they saw it germinate, grow and blossom in her eyes.

One of the men had found an unoccupied stool: sitting on it, he raised his legs so that his feet reached right up to the bar. 'Hey, take those boots off there!' the barman shouted. 'It's all right, I'm quite comfortable,' the man replied. Taking a small mouth organ from his pocket he began to play snatches from tunes. From time to time some of the men would recognise one and join in.

The handsome soldier in the red coat had rested his arms on Marie's shoulders and was gently, without any ulterior motive, playing with the curls that lay beneath the nape of her neck. Outside stretched a fine winter landscape, great expanses of meadow in which slender trees rose up towards a heavy grey sky. The trees were very tall and almost purple in colour, and their leafless silhouettes were filled out with round dark clusters. One soldier dug another with his elbow and said: 'Look, Pierre, there's some mistletoe – doesn't it look pretty!'

And from all this arose a strange, wonderful, almost sorrowful meaning, a sorrow untouched by grief. It came from the voices, the gestures, the faces, the landscape. It came from the sound of the glasses, and from the sound of the train; from the songs and from the men's laughter; perhaps even from the colour of the uniforms and of Marie's own dress. It came from little things as much as from big things, and it rose up in Marie, enveloping her and making her catch her breath. She felt that even the slightest increase in the link between her and all of these things would make her dizzy to the point of vertigo; that she would die of excitement if the word that defines these specific meanings were ever to be uttered.

AT THE END OF THE JOURNEY there would be this immense brightness. Her heart was pounding, in big, deep beats, keeping up with the dull rhythm of the train. It was going fast now, and the kilometres were diminishing … The stations they passed were now carrying fine French names (almost too fine and too French): Lonecourt, Ernoxeville, la Ferté-Grande, Landelin-le-Duc …

As she left the carriage the men grabbed her hands and told her their names. There was no point in them doing this, but it gave them pleasure and it seemed like a proof of friendship: 'Pierre Malinoï', 'René Binet', 'Sébastien Rémy', 'Jules Bottin', 'Marcel Cabillot'.

'And my name is Marie,' she said.

'Marie what?'

She looked at them: the little black one with very deep-set eyes, the redhead with the face of a child, the lieutenant who seemed younger than ever in his smart jacket, the one with a pretty voice who had spoken to Pierre, the blond with a big nose and a flat face, the tall dark hungry-looking one who played the mouth organ, and the magnificent African soldier. She smiled at them all and shrugged her shoulders: 'Just Marie.'

They said goodbye one more time, calling her by her first name, and sang two verses of a song which began: 'Farewell, dear comrade, farewell, we must part!'

Back in the carriage where Marie had left her book and her coat, all the seats were still full. In the corridor, to one side of the door, a woman sat on a black case. On the other side a man in a cap was sitting on a kit-bag; he was either her husband or her brother. Between them was a bored, miserable child. Unlike Marie, they were not getting off at the next big station: when the child asked when they would arrive at their destination, the woman replied: 'Oh, a long time yet!'

The woman's gestures were small, whether she was pulling the two edges of her coat together or adjusting her hair. She had a joyless face and frightened eyes; she held her arms too tightly against her body and her hands too closely together, as if she wanted to prevent her unhappiness from deserting her. Everything she said to the child was mournful – there was always misfortune in her voice – and the sadness of the mother transferred to the child.

A soldier walked along the corridor, with all his gear, and Marie leaned against the wall of the carriage to let him pass. He was carrying a bag with a pair of big studded boots attached to it and as he went past they knocked the child's head, lightly scratching his cheek.

The child didn't want to complain; he simply wanted some consolation for what had happened. His thoughts turned to the bread and sausage which his mother had brought with them in the case and which he'd been looking forward to for hours. He said: 'I'm hungry …'

'It's not mealtime yet,' she replied.

The tone of her voice suggested that this was something distressing that she could do nothing about. The child felt the tears beginning to come and since everything was so sad and dismal anyway, went up to his mother to show her his forehead and his cheek. She took his head in her hands and said: 'You've been hurt …'

He was truly hungry, and now he knew that he had been hurt, too. Lowering his head he threw himself upon his mother, and cried, distraught, into her miserable lap. She lifted him up so that he could be closer to her, pressed his head to her chest, and put her arms around him. Speaking in her sad voice, she consoled him with words far more painful than the minor discomfort he was going through. She smothered and enveloped him, holding him against her, against the pain inside her.

Marie would have liked to take the child away – anywhere, as long as it was far from his mother.

He cried even harder. The man, emerging from his half-sleep, took stock of the situation. 'Come here, I'll show you something.'

'What?'

'We're going to play cards.'

The child stood up, holding his breath, suddenly uncertain whether to laugh or weep. The man lightly patted the scratched cheek, to show him it wasn't worth crying about – and also to give him some sense of the agony and anxiety of daily life: the boredom of waiting for things and the bargain you make with misfortune. The child decided to laugh, sitting on the kit-bag next to him and starting to deal the cards.

Marie smiled at the man and the child then went back to the window of the train. It was going so fast now! They were almost there, only another half-hour to go. Her heart was beating very, very quickly. She gradually calmed herself down by looking at the fine landscape outside the window.

IT IS STARTING TO SNOW: a light dusting that barely covers the woods, or the paths, where the earth is brown and the big russet-coloured fields undulate gently at the far edge of the landscape. No village, no house, no other colour, nothing but a light covering of snow on the fields; but the waviness of the landscape makes these big expanses of wild plants seem either darker or lighter than they really are. Marie watches as all the browns and all the russets die and are born again.

The landscape changes, its place taken by the flat line of a canal, with houses, roads, sounds. Cars pass by on a viaduct, and people stop to watch the great train as it slows down below them. All at once, a metal plaque on the station announces a place that is imbued with the full power of reality.

CHAPTER NINETEEN

H E WALKS FAST and Marie keeps pace, following him
into a square and on to streets which resemble the
outskirts of any station. He starts to walk more slowly as
the singular nature of the town begins to become apparent,
so that Marie can appreciate it. It is dark but not yet night,
and in the gentle half-light the façades of the buildings have
a handsome, strange and solitary air. They belong to another
century, and they have a magnificently pure style, sometimes
lining up in immensely broad avenues, sometimes grouping
together into squares that are fine, calm, disdainful.

Marie allows herself be led. They cross semicircles composed of colonnades, palaces and arcades; they pass bronze gates
edged with gold. They follow a wide boulevard, then a narrower
one that looks like a garden, decorated with fountains and
planted with clumps of trees broken up by arc-shaped doors.

He hasn't planned this route, there was nothing in particular he wanted to show her – the whole town is like this. With its silent, fixed beauty, with its face of stone and gold, it summons up an important period in history. For Marie, it is the finest town in France.

NIGHT HAS WELL AND TRULY fallen now, and covers the gates, the avenues, the fountains. In the park where they are walking, only one path is lit up and the remainder, lying in darkness, seems vast, secret.

Realising that Marie left Paris in the morning, he suggests they stop for an early dinner. The menu contains names that are new to her: dishes change from one region to another. He orders the local wine. The vineyards around here are too scarce to have any serious commercial value, and the wine is drunk only in the area.

No doubt he has been to this restaurant before and the people know him, or perhaps it's because, sitting opposite each other, they look so young: the waiters call her 'Mademoiselle'. He tells her a bit about the courses he is taking, the things he is learning, the books he is reading. Marie watches him and, without him knowing what she is doing, caresses him with her gaze. She would very much like to say more: is it the richness of the moment that inspires her silence? She is silent because she is overwhelmed by happiness. He is there, she is there: no one can tell whether that will lead to gentleness or to violence. Their happiness has the cruel value of something brief and intense. And yet it is only a dawning: they have the whole evening and the whole night before them, and since they see each other so little, one hour spent together has the richness of a whole day.

Time spent like this still passes too quickly, and it is now eleven o'clock: the town is asleep. They pass under an ancient gate fortified with turrets, beautiful and massive in the night; their steps echo under the arches. One long avenue to go: he takes her arm, squeezes it a little and, still holding her, leads her to where he lives. At the threshold of his room, Marie has the sense of finally penetrating to the heart of this hand-some, secretive town.

The room is small, the wallpaper decorated with minute stylised flowers, very close together. The table is covered in books and coursework and some wooden skis are propped up against the wardrobe, their curved ends standing away from it. An open folding screen reveals a washbasin, and a light rain-coat hangs from a peg on a coat stand. There is a print of a Rouault painting: pinkish tones which brighten and soften on the face of a very human-looking Christ. And a Degas, with a strangely green ballet dancer. A low bed is covered in cretonne, the same material that covers each side of the window. Marie's eyes travel from one object to another, loving every one.

They ate so early that they are hungry again. From a shelf in the wardrobe he takes some bread, butter and apples, and they sit next to each other, eating amongst the books. Something primitive flows alongside the blood in Marie's veins: she experiences a special womanly joy at cutting bread for him and buttering it.

They talk a little more. When Marie stands up, very near the table where she has put down an exercise book he is showing her, he suddenly takes her in his arms, and they begin to talk like two people who have just greeted each other.

THEY ARE STRETCHED OUT across the bed next to each other. Marie, her head thrown back, sees yet another Degas print: a circle of short tulle skirts on a bench, with heads looking down at satin slippers. She looks around her again. How light and peaceful this room is! No doubt other women have come here, and others would come after …

All at once Marie encircles his knees with her leg like a she-animal and throws herself across his body as if to defend it from another. Jealous she-animal, the primitive blood in her veins … She quickly rejects this shameful emotion, for it threatens to overshadow the only thing that really matters: that he is here, she is here, and today is today.

He is lying on his back and she is curled up against him. Her hands are beneath his arms and she is holding him by the shoulders. His arms are around her, hands clasped in the small of her back. They lie in this embrace for a long time, letting the tenderness well up inside.

MUCH LATER, after the lights in the room have gone out, they are lying some way apart from each other. In the middle of the space that separates them, the left hand of one and the right hand of the other meet. Perhaps they are asleep. The lights in the road outside project the outline of the venetian blinds on to the walls in long golden stripes. The silence in this room is absolute; and outside, too, apart from the far-off whistle of a fast train to Paris. A train that does not contain Marie ...

One hand has moved, clasping the other more tightly to show that he wasn't asleep. Marie's eyes shine brightly in the darkness. Her gaze loses itself in the bright outlines of the room, and she dreams, almost to the point of sleep. He is beside me. He who is so like me, strong and silent. And I am still myself, more than ever myself. Those broad stripes of light: they stretch up to the ceiling and on to the walls, almost in the shape of a chapel ... Saint Marie of Solitude. Our Lady has found her heart, her fine, hard heart that no blade can pierce. Her heart is so big that it needs to be protected by broad, high, golden gates, in the shape of a chapel ...

Marie has closed her eyes. Their hands have slipped apart and, with a light sigh of happiness, their bodies join up again in a double circle of arms.

At last they sleep. But when the pale light of dawn replaces the stripes of light, they want to make love again, for a long time, right up to the moment when they get up and prepare to leave.

Standing in front of the window Marie discovers what she is about to leave behind. On the avenue, almost opposite the window, stands a triumphal arch with three gates supporting a number of heavy stone ornaments. At the very top of her sightline she sees shields, armour and frozen banners and, on the haut-reliefs, horses standing high amongst brandished arms and helmeted warriors. On top of the old facades, granite balconies display coats of arms emblazoned with weapons, fleurs-de-lis, ducal crowns, and sculpted vases with heavy stone foliage held up by cupids. The view extends further: two cathedral spires rise above the houses and, over the rooftops all around the town, soft brown hills climb towards the sky.

She turns away from the window and he says softly: 'Are you ready? Perhaps we could find time to have breakfast before your train leaves …'

She moves closer to him; he holds her by the shoulders and looks at her for a moment. On the lapel of his jacket she sees the little metal badge shining close to her eyes. She puts her hand on it and rests her head on the lapel, concealing her quivering face in the crook of his shoulder. At last she finds the strength to raise her head and they look at each other again.

'You have such beautiful eyes …'

So soft was the voice, like a whispering from mouth to mouth, that it could have come from either of them.

Outside, in the freezing air of the avenue, they walk along with their customary brisk step in their customary silence, their expressions once more impassive and hard. In the light of morning, the town is whiter, calmer, even more proudly handsome than the night before. As they cross a square, some purple pigeons fly up. There is still snow on the clipped trees. Marie looks at the trees: with their naked branches, so tightly interwoven, it's hard to know whether they are elms, hornbeams or limes. When they sprout leaves, perhaps she will be able to tell.

CHAPTER TWENTY

THEY HAD ALREADY PARTED; the platform was full of noise and movement. It was easy to distinguish between those who were embarking on a big journey and those who were only waiting for trains to outlying districts, and you could tell whether they were sad or happy and what work they did – you could read something of their lives on their faces.

But these two made no sign at all, and nothing in their demeanour recalled the hours they had just spent together: you would have said that they had no future.

The train has arrived, an attendant has called out. Their hands barely touched, and to see them you would not know whether they were greeting each other or separating. The doors closed, and he retreated along the platform, with his big calm gait. You couldn't see his face, you didn't know what he was thinking.

Marie stayed for a moment in the shadow of the corridor, standing very straight, teeth clenched. Behind the window, everything unfurled backwards: the great iron viaduct, the road that followed the track, the houses and gardens, the canal.

She sits in a third-class compartment and the minutes go by, merging into one. As they pass through the reality of landscapes and villages, the distance increases according to the relentless rhythm of the wheels. It's already snowing on the russet-coloured fields, and over there, far away, lies the handsome town, a little to the right or a little to the left, fixed in its circle of rolling hills. A small island of reality in the bigger reality of the world.

On the seat opposite a child, waking too quickly, rubs his eyes and whimpers. A woman is endlessly searching for something in a big leather bag. A soldier sleeps, legs stretched out: in a movement beyond his control, his hand supports his head, then abandons it, then returns to support it once again. A young girl is eating an orange. Marie is sitting in the corner near the window, hands crossed, head leaning on the wood of the compartment. Her clothes and her whole body retain the smell of love.

CHAPTER TWENTY-ONE

'OH NO, NOT MILK! I can't bear any more milk! What I'd really like is an orange juice ...'

Marie put the warm milk down on the table and began to squeeze some fruit.

Claudine was still very pale but her eyes were clearer.

'One sugar, two sugars, ten sugars, fifty sugars?'

Laughing loudly, Claudine replied: 'Not even one, I'm too thirsty!'

She drank it down like a child, then handed the empty glass back to Marie.

'That was delicious; I'm so glad you've come back.' Sitting up straighter against her pillow she tapped the edge of the bed. 'Come and sit down, close to me,' she said.

Taking Marie's hands in hers, as she always did, she looked at her: 'What is that I see in your eyes?'

'What do you mean?'

Claudine seemed worried, almost sad, and tried to explain herself: 'There's a sort of light there; I don't know what it is … It's in your walk and in your gestures as well. Almost as if you had come into bloom. And yet you don't look any older, far from it.'

A big, calm, sweet smile spread over Marie's face as Claudine repeated flatly: 'I don't know what it can be.'

Moving closer to her sister she reached out, her hands nearly grabbing Marie's shoulder. 'Tell me, what have you been doing? Where have you been?'

Marie went on smiling. She stroked Claudine's hair with both hands, each side of the pathetic, doll-like face.

But Claudine went on talking, her lips almost touching Marie's face, her miserable mouth and her feverish breath saying: 'Tell me, so that I can do the same thing as you …'

In a movement that was too abrupt for Claudine's invalid arms, Marie got up.

She stands by the bed, her smile suddenly dead, and looks at Claudine.

'You know how much I need you, Marie; you mustn't go off on your own.'

'But I am here again now, I've come back.'

'No, Marie, you haven't come back.'

Stretching her hands out again she takes refuge in Marie's arms and begins to weep softly.

'Come back, Marie, and tell me about it …'

'I have nothing to tell. Life isn't a story to be told like

that. At the very most it might be something that could be shown …'

'But if my eyes don't see?'

'You only see what you can understand. And you only understand what you love. First you have to give yourself, commit, then you'll receive something in exchange. But you, you're always waiting, waiting for something to turn up. You don't know what it's called, it's just a vague sort of happiness which might come to you suddenly and overwhelm you. And because nothing turned up, you got desperate and decided you wanted to die. But everything was there waiting for you. It's up to you to love, up to you to live. Making the most of life is making the most of yourself …'

Marie was probably only speaking for herself – this was not something that Claudine could understand. But Claudine became calmer as she leaned against her sister's breast. Words and flesh full of light and heat, enveloping her … She was being healed by her contact with Marie's passionate peace.

Marie held her against her, then put her to bed, pulling the blankets up high so she wouldn't feel the cold

'When are you going back to Maubeuge?'

'Tomorrow morning.'

'And you'll come and see me tonight?'

'Yes.'

CHAPTER TWENTY-TWO

WHEN MARIE LEFT she went to the home of a pupil who was expecting her, and worked with him until midday. Her next class didn't start till three, so she had a long moment of freedom ahead of her.

ONE HOUR AMONGST OTHERS. All hours are precious, but the value of this one comes from the fact that she is spending it alone. At this moment any other known presence would disturb her.

It isn't cold, but neither is there any winter sun. The air is colourless: there is nothing to brighten the streets or make them sad, and the houses retain the hue of the stones they are made of. Everything presents itself just as it is. Marie walks slowly, with an easy step. Calm, pensive and alone, she considers the faces that are in her heart.

Jean: how much has changed in the tender halo that emanates from your face! I realise that there is no god on high to protect the love between a woman and her husband: no word has even been invented to describe it. Friendship, tenderness, love, passion, desire – none of them are suitable, they all signify something else, so I will leave unnamed the human, only human feelings which occupy that place in my heart. So many things have changed and yet so many have remained the same, truer perhaps than the ones that went before, and more alive than ever. I do know that today, on this day, I desire you less, but that may simply be a stage in the love I have for you. I know, too, that I will never cease to love you. And I know that if you asked me to, I would follow you to the end of the world.

Claudine: my sad sister – her face, how it worries me! And yet it stays in my heart. I shall go back to see her tonight, then tomorrow I shall go to Maubeuge. You don't find freedom by giving people up: freedom comes from the very core of what you did not forsake. Departures and arrivals, and then fresh departures … When I leave, it isn't to run away, it's to move towards something else.

And you, that other face, so young, so tough, so distant: your beautiful smooth face leaning over me, your eyelids with their long lashes on which I have placed my lips, the hair that I have caressed with my hands. Are you the face of love? A question I don't need to answer – one feels one's emotions, one doesn't have to explain them in words.

You are a long way away from me, and I accept that

painful distance. I do not know exactly in what way you love me. Don't tell me. Spare me your life, keep it to yourself: you have the right to do so. And if you did not have that right, you would need to acquire it. As for me – I love you, but I shan't tell you so, I shall say it to myself. Why should I curb it when I feel it so powerfully? I love you. I might love you for a short time, I might love you forever – no one knows.

In love, neither perfection nor eternity is predetermined. Love operates according to the pulse of time, just like everything else that lives. It asserts itself or disintegrates, it goes into decline, recovers its strength. If it's alive, then it can die – and that is beautiful in itself. Nothing can ever be important or have the power to move unless it contains within itself the possibility of death. Struggles and safeguards, combined struggles of the heart and the flesh; the success or failure of any one hour in relation to the one that came before it; taking risks, moving forward step by step.

Does an eternal, perfect love have perpetual beauty? Does a love that dies have tragic beauty? Does a newborn love have blinding beauty? For me, a different kind of beauty is preferable to all of those – a beauty that is neither perpetual nor tragic nor blinding, but heavy, difficult and real. It's the beauty of love not at the moment of birth or of death but at the moment of life.

I am at a stage when I love you, the handsome face that I see in my heart. Will I see you again? Trains, trains and more trains: steel tracks will shine in my life like star points. After every encounter we must part without tears and without saying goodbye. We must part without promises and without clasped hands, because our love is a living thing.

All those faces I see in my heart ...

Is that all, or is there something else? A big, anonymous, living face that even the most ardent of my other loves can no longer eclipse, composed of a quantity of people, of things, of gestures, of landscapes – the great face of the world, marked by joy and suffering, by blessings and miseries. Most of all, on that beloved face, nothing changes: everything is so beautiful just as it is.

These reflections brought Marie to a halt. She stood stock still on the corner of a Paris street, with dreamy eyes and a broad smile.

In the road two workmen were setting up the boundaries of a zebra crossing; they worked bent over the ground, which was giving off a strong smell of bitumen. One of them looked up and asked her: 'What is it, my lovely; are you laughing at the angels?'

He bent over the ground again and Marie responded, to herself rather than to him: 'Actually I'm smiling at you.'

Just as she smiled at all the gentle people who passed. at two children who lingered to look at her, satchels under their arms; at a woman in a hurry; at a young soldier who had no desire for victory of any kind: at all these gentle people touched by the simple grace of being alive.

TRANSLATOR'S AFTERWORD

WHEN *MARIE* WAS PUBLISHED in French in 1943, it was entitled *A la Recherche de Marie*: at its heart lies the sensuous fusion of immediate experience and recovered memory so effectively captured by Marcel Proust, a writer whom Madeleine Bourdouxhe much admired. For today's feminist readers, familiar with a European tradition, its single-minded exploration of a woman's psyche may carry additional echoes: of Virginia Woolf or Jean Rhys, or of Marguerite Duras. And despite that formal homage to *A la Recherche du temps perdu*, the writing of Madeleine Bourdouxhe is so distinctive as to make one continually wary of placing her within any literary tradition, even a modernist one.

This startling singularity, combined with political circum-stance and a certain authorial diffidence, explains almost half a century of neglect. *Marie* is the third of Bourdouxhe's works to be translated into English. She began to be reprinted in France and Belgium in the mid-1980s. A volume of short stories, *A Nail, a Rose*, first appeared in English in 1989, followed by the novella, *La Femme de Gilles*, in 1992 (republished by Daunt Books in 2015). She died in April 1996, five months before her ninetieth birthday.

The resurgence of interest in her work brought her some gratification but no great surprise. In my conversations with her, which began in 1988 when I was translating the short stories, I came to realise that she had always retained a sense of her literary value. In her own highly developed private world she was sure of her identity as a professional author. She had never stopped writing, but she was not greatly concerned about widespread recognition, knowing that her main literary engagement must be with her own fictional creations rather than with publishers or even readers.

Although my questions were answered with great warmth and politeness, Bourdouxhe was never forthcoming about her life, reserving the right to disdain almost all connection between it and her work: 'That is what writers do – they invent.' Of *A la Recherche de Marie*, she said only that the chief similarity between herself and Marie was that 'we were both married women'.

Even so, it was possible to piece together a biographical outline, at least up to the time when *A la Recherche de Marie* was published. In the beginning, success came easily. The positive critical response to Gallimard's publication of *La Femme de Gilles* (1937), published when she was thirty, gave her an instant place among the up-and-coming novelists of the day, along with Simone de Beauvoir and Nathalie Sarraute. From an early age – she was born in 1906 – she had made up her mind to be a writer. As a small child her main literary influence was her adored Liégeois grandfather, who instilled in her a love of the French poets and philosophers. It was in Liège, too, that she developed her fascination for the minutiae of working-class life, spending much of her time with the family's maidservant. In our conversations she gave me the impression of a comfortable but isolated childhood in which she was an only child until a sister was born in 1915 and a brother in 1921.

In 1914 her father's work took the family to Paris, where they lived for the entire period of World War I. This left an indelible impression on the young Madeleine's imagination that is surely reflected in the many striking vignettes of Paris in *Marie*, where the charm of the city – boulevards, cafés, stations, squares and *petits coins* alike – is evoked in a particularly haunting way. 'It was Paris,' she declared, 'that formed my true childhood memories.'

After the family's return to Brussels she entered the fifth form at the Lycée. 'I lived in a bourgeois ambience: my father was a businessman, my mother spent a lot of time with nuns, and they weren't interested in literature. They let me decide what to do. I studied Latin, French, American literature – then spent two years reading philosophy at the University of Brussels.'

As Bourdouxhe recalled them, these were years of intense intellectual excitement: 'We formed a little group, four or five of us, all set on going in a different direction from our teachers. We were interested in what came from within ourselves, and in what we discovered through chance reading in bookshops. No one in our families, or at university, guided us – we yielded to no authority. We chose our own aesthetic and our only influences were Nietzsche, Gide and Apollinaire.'

In 1927 Bourdouxhe married a mathematics teacher, Jacques Muller. For the first few years of the marriage she gave Latin and French lessons at home and at a private school. 'My main preoccupation was always literature and writing – that was my chief aim. But I wrote neither poetry, fiction nor essays: I was expecting a novel.' In 1934 she started an apprentice work, *Vacances*, a version of which was published in a Belgian anarchist magazine, *Le Rouge et le noir*, in 1936. She began *La Femme de Gilles* at the end of 1935 and completed it in June 1936, taking the manuscript in November to the Paris offices of the literary magazine, *La Nouvelle Revue Française*. In 1937, the year that *La Femme de Gilles* was published by Gallimard, she started work on *A la Recherche de Marie*. Although it is not overtly a political novel, the threat of World War II, and the atmosphere of confusion that preceded it, hangs in the air. War was declared soon after the manuscript was completed, followed by the occupation of France and Belgium.

From now on Bourdouxhe played an informal part in the resistance movement, sheltering Jewish refugees and British airmen and, on one occasion, taking important documents to Paul Eluard in Paris. She told the Brussels magazine, *Bulletin*, in 1989: 'We all helped, the whole neighbourhood. When the Gestapo came looking for anyone, there was a pre-arranged escape route through the back gardens. We knew it was dangerous but it was the only thing to do.'

Her political consciousness had already been raised by the Spanish Civil War and by her friendship with the Russian revolutionary writer Victor Serge, whom she also harboured in Brussels. She was deeply affected by the war, and the reality of the occupation: she once saw an American woman killed in the street. Such experiences had a lasting effect on the short stories she was now writing. But publication and the life of a professional writer were beginning to seem less relevant. In 1940 she gave birth to her only child, Marie, days before Belgium was invaded. (She evokes her escape to France from the nursing home, baby in arms, in the short story 'Sous le Pont Mirabeau', its title a tribute to Apollinaire.)

By now she had turned her back on the Paris literary scene, where many publishers had been taken over by the Nazis. Eventually she published *A la Recherche de Marie* with a small Brussels press, Editions Libris, in 1943. She described Libris as 'above suspicion', by which she meant uncontaminated by fascism.

When the war was over she started to make regular visits to Paris, where she would spend time in literary cafés with Raymond Queneau, Jean-Paul Sartre and Simone de Beauvoir. Sartre published one of her stories in *Les Temps Modernes* and de Beauvoir, who became a friend, was a consistent admirer. She identified two recurring themes in Bourdouxhe's work: her acute perception of the chasm that can open up between men and women immediately after the sexual act, and her enduring interest in the special relationship between women and material objects, particularly in the kitchen ('the nest'). The passage in which Marie reflects upon 'the mutual understanding between the palms of her hands and the objects they touch' inspired a long disquisition on the subject in *Le Deuxième Sexe* (1949). Housework, de Beauvoir suggests, is for many the 'social justification' of their existence, an enriching activity that confirms their status in the world. The completion of a domestic task – washing linen or polishing a table – constitutes the active fulfilment of a dream, since the negative (the dirty object) has been replaced by the positive (the clean one). De Beauvoir cites the intense pleasure felt by Marie as she cleans her stove: 'The well-polished steel sends her back a reflection of the freedom and power she feels at the very tips of her fingers.' When Marie sees herself in the stove she has so meticulously scoured, she and the stove become contiguous, or mirror images of each other.

The several mentions of Bourdouxhe in *Le Deuxième Sexe* I had to discover for myself: the information was not volunteered, though she was pleased to be reminded of it, and it prompted other memories of her post-war life, when she had some involvement in the artistic *milieu* of Brussels, mixing with the painters René Magritte and Paul Delvaux and discussing with them the Surrealist ideas that were already so striking a feature of her literary style. She eventually became '*secrétaire perpetuelle*' of the 'alternative' Libre Académie de Belgique.

Several of Bourdouxhe's stories appeared in French and Belgian magazines during the 1940s and 1950s but *A la Recherche de Marie* was the last novel to be published until her rediscovery in the 1980s. (An experiment in historical fantasy, *Mantoue est trop loin*, was submitted to Gallimard and Grasset but never appeared.) By the end of the twentieth century most of her oeuvre was available in several languages, and in 2009 an international conference was held in Paris to celebrate her life and work.*

Whilst the power of Bourdouxhe's earlier novel, *La Femme de Gilles*, derives from its tragic inevitability, *Marie* resonates

---

* The book of the proceedings is the first comprehensive tribute to the writer's achievements: *Relire Madeleine Bourdouxhe: Regards croisés sur son œuvre littéraire*, eds. Cécile Kovacshazy et Christiane Solte-Gresser, Bruxelles: Peter Lang, 2011.

with female energy and optimism. In *La Femme de Gilles* a young mother commits suicide because she falls out of love with her husband after he has an affair with her sister. By contrast Marie, who has not yet decided whether to have children, takes a lover for herself and finds liberation through her own actions, making the book a true text for our times.

In the very first chapter Bourdouxhe takes us, characteristically, to the depths of the heroine's heart and soul. She shows us a thirty-year-old woman overflowing with love, not just for her husband but for the whole of humanity and for inanimate objects, too: a boat in the harbour, a scattering of light on the sea, a hotel balcony, a cigarette. Marie is revealed as a woman with an interior life so highly charged and discrete that she is in a continual state of euphoria, as yet finding fulfilment only in her fantasy life. Her husband, Jean, is fond of her but – as he himself half realises – cannot match her intensity.

In the blinding heat of a Côte d'Azur afternoon Marie and Jean make their way to the beach; Marie is in a trance-like state. While Jean is in the water she exchanges a meaningful look with a boy she sees lying on the beach. In the work of Bourdouxhe, sexual desire is always non-negotiable. Just as the fatal course of *La Femme de Gilles* is determined by the illicit kiss in the first scene, so for Marie there is now no turning back. The damage – or in this case, the awakening – cannot be reversed. But this is a journey that Marie is more than ready for: the relationship she already knows she will have with the unnamed boy will give her the freedom to delve deep into her unconscious self and rebuild it with the manifold possibilities that erotic love can offer. It will help her reanimate the abandon of her youth; it will enlarge her whole world.

The feelings aroused by the boy give Marie a new confidence, a yearning for her lost independence. She escapes from Jean and his chattering companions and takes a boat out to sea, rowing alone for the first time in her life. If Jean were here he would take charge, but he is not. 'He is of less concern to her now than the sea, the boat and its oars … It's as though she can see the colour of the water in the night, and breathe the smell that rises up from it, for the first time in years. At that moment she is alone.' This is remarkably reminiscent of the scene in Kate Chopin's *The Awakening* (1899), another rediscovered classic of women's writing, in which the heroine Edna, inspired by her first sensual experience with Robert, swims out into the sea. 'A feeling of exultation overtook her, as if some power of significant import had been given her to control the working of her body and her soul. She would not join the groups in their sports and bouts, but intoxicated with her newly conquered power, she swam out alone.'

Marie and *The Awakening* are both unusually open in their descriptions of sexual passion, and both heroines are insistent upon their entitlement to 'alternative lives'. It would be as unthinkable for Bourdouxhe's Marie to discuss her new state of mind with Jean as it would be for Chopin's Edna to show either 'shame or remorse' at her behaviour: 'She had all her life long been accustomed to harbour thoughts and emotions which never voiced themselves. They had never taken the form of struggles. They belonged to her and were her own, and she entertained the conviction that she had a right to them and that they concerned no one but herself.'

Back on shore, Marie's private journey has begun, and so has the prolonged Proustian process of searching for her identity through memory. As she starts to free herself from the shackles of submissive femininity, she finds she is 'lost between two shattered worlds', with all its consequences – including the possible loss of both lovers. Her thoughts wander. In the enchanting scene where she is trying to teach Latin to a reluctant teenage boy, she recalls previous loves, her student life at the Sorbonne, and the way in which her early marriage, though outwardly contented, has circumscribed her. She has become a protective creature, self-absorbed and inward-looking, whose life is bounded by her husband, her feckless sister Claudine, and her parents. She longs for release, of the kind that the Renaissance poet Louise Labé seems to offer – she herself has few friends, as she finds most other women tedious. She is progressing towards a series of moments that will free her of the reins she has, until now, held too tightly to herself.

These heightened moments can either be triggered by a tenuous link between present and past – like the flood of familiar sensations that invade Marcel while he is listening to music towards the end of the last volume of *A la Recherche du temps perdu* – or directly attributable to a specific feeling that brings with it an urgent reminder of a previous one (the madeleine dipped in tea, first at Combray and later in Paris) Like Marcel, Marie experiences both types of recovered memory. Dreams of her past sometimes invade her consciousness without her knowing why, except perhaps that she is in a mood to receive them; at other times, the link is clear, as in the scene at her parents' house in Neuilly, after she has seen Jean off on the train to Maubeuge.

She arrives earlier than usual, and is delighted to find them eating breakfast, her mother still wearing a hairnet – something she hasn't seen for some time. In her current state of emotional turmoil she seeks reassurance in the familiar comforts of her childhood home, and she is amply rewarded. She asks for the hot chocolate that her father customarily drinks – cocoa without milk – and revels in the taste and feel of the insipid liquid as it trickles down her throat. The feelings evoked by the drink are at once vague, all-encompassing, and sharp, specific; they are essentially rooted in the familial, in a poignant remembrance of childhood that will give new meaning to the life of an adult. Marie goes on to trick her mother into mispronouncing a neighbour's name and reminisces with her about the past as they share the household tasks. She is drawing her mother out and drawing comfort from her at the same time. She is in complete control.

This control, this loftiness, sets Marie apart from other Bourdouxe heroines. She shares many qualities with Elisa of *La Femme de Gilles* – her tenderness, her strength of will and her need for silence. But unlike Elisa, Marie has intellectual resources to draw on: even at moments of special intensity (often conveyed in the present tense) she retains the capacity to analyse, to interpret her experience, to make decisions. In a fascinating inversion, possibly prompted by the hostility Bourdouxhe encountered from a few women for 'allowing' Elisa to take her own life, in *Marie* it is the other type of woman – flirtatious, careless and talkative – who attempts suicide.

The rights and wrongs of suicide occupy much of the latter part of the novel, as though Bourdouxhe feels compelled to continue the debate, to assure her readers that she takes the issue with due seriousness. Marie has come to feel superior to her sister Claudine, and in spite of her genuine anxiety about whether she will survive, works herself into a fury as she rushes to her sickbed: 'It's all refusal, all along the way! When women suffer, what do they do? Cut their losses, that's what. A cowardly flight towards peace, towards annihilation ... You must not desert; you must be on the side of life.' Guessing that Marie is hiding something, Claudine begs her to confess, but Marie denies her: 'Life isn't a story to be told like that ... Making the most of life is making the most of yourself.'

Marie's sense of being on a higher plane can occasionally tip over unto unsociability. At such times Bourdouxhe employs the deft narrative device of passing the ball to another character, as if to give us the chance to assess her behaviour objectively: to Jean, in Maubeuge, when Marie fails to conceal her dismay at the dingy domesticity of his parents' house – 'God, she's difficult' – and to the Sartrean womaniser Marius Denis, when she shows contempt for his clumsy seduction technique and his pretentious plans for a woman's magazine: 'two spoonfuls of Spinoza, one of Plato, three grams of Bergson'. She is harsh on Marius, effectively attempting to demolish his whole *raison d'être*, but instead of defending himself he is reduced to a state of silent admiration for her unusually spirited discourse; at this point we see Marie quite clearly through his eyes. It takes an author in supreme command of her characters to shift the narrative thrust so abruptly at two of the most dramatic moments in her novel.

The final word rests with Marie herself, who is by now so free and so at one with the terms of her own existence that she lives permanently in awe of Pascal's 'infinite spaces', acutely aware of her infinitesimal part in the universe. At several moments in this novel Marie is truly alone: when she looks up at the thunder above the mountains and imagines herself 'rushing down those dry slopes, looking up at the flashing light, her face pitched against the cold, hard storm'; when, at the very end, she stands smiling on the corner of a Paris street – watching and being watched.

Faith Evans

January 2016

Daunt Books

Founded in 2010, the Daunt Books imprint
is dedicated to discovering brilliant works
by talented authors from around the world.
Whether reissuing beautiful new editions
of lost classics or introducing fresh literary
voices, we're drawn to writing that evokes a
strong sense of place – novels, short fiction,
memoirs, travel accounts and translations
with a lingering atmosphere, a thrilling story,
and a distinctive style. With our roots as a
travel bookshop, the titles we publish are
inspired by the Daunt shops themselves,
and the exciting atmosphere of discovery to
be found in a good bookshop.

For more information, please visit
www.dauntbookspublishing.co.uk